PARANORMAL SCIENCE NVL
Occultic;Nine
オカルティック・ナイン
THERE IS NO SUCH THING AS THE "OCCULT." IT CAN ALL BE DISPROVED BY SCIENCE.
ONLY THOSE WHO HAVE ACCEPTED EVERYTHING
HAVE THE RIGHT TO KNOW THE TRUTH.
02
CHIYOMARU SHIKURA
art by pako
D0546429
orz

⟨Death is
something
that's given
to the chosen.
And you still
ain't got
that right.⟩

*"Heheh...
heheheh...
I knew it.
You're
my devil.
My own,
personal
devil..."*

"Gamo, are you talking about that again...?"

"Oh, this thing talks all the time."

"Th-this is..."

It felt like the lock on it
matched the gold tooth key.

PARANORMAL SCIENCE NVL

Occultic;Nine

オカルティック・ナイン

THERE IS NO SUCH THING AS THE "OCCULT." IT CAN ALL BE DISPROVED BY SCIENCE.
ONLY THOSE WHO HAVE ACCEPTED EVERYTHING
HAVE THE RIGHT TO KNOW THE TRUTH.

02

Presented by
CHIYOMARU SHIKURA

Illustrated by
pako

OCCULTIC;NINE, VOLUME 2

Illustrations by pako

First published in Japan in 2015 by
OVERLAP Inc., Ltd., Tokyo.
English translation rights arranged with
OVERLAP Inc., Ltd., Tokyo.

Translation: Adam Lensenmayer
J-Novel Editors: Alicia Ashby and Sasha McGlynn
Book Layout: Karis Page
Cover Design: Nicky Lim
Copy Editor: Tom Speelman
Light Novel Editor: Jenn Grunigen
Production Assistant: CK Russell
Production Manager: Lissa Pattillo
Editor-in-Chief: Adam Arnold
Publisher: Jason DeAngelis

ISBN: 978-1-626926-61-5
Printed in Canada
First Printing: September 2017
10 9 8 7 6 5 4 3 2 1

CONTENTS

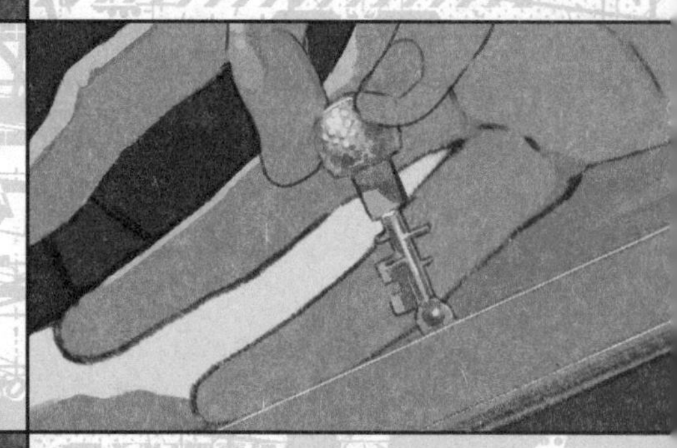

超常科学NVL
Occultic;Nine
オカルティック・ナイン
THERE ARE NO SUCH THING AS "OCCULT". IT CAN BE DISPROVED ALL BY SCIENCE.
ONLY THE ONES WHO HAVE ACCEPTED EVERYTHING
CAN GET THE RIGHT TO KNOW THE TRUTH.

▶ site 25: Yuta Gamon ——— 2/24 (Wednesday)

The edge of the knife in my hands glistened a slick red. I wasn't sure if that red was the color of the knife itself or the color of the blood.

I laughed.

I laughed very naturally. I tried to hold it back, and it turned into a chuckle.

"Heh...heheheh... gwahah..." I laughed a creepy laugh as I stabbed the red knife into Dr. Hashigami's chest again and again. I could feel the dull sensation of ripping flesh beneath my hands. It was terrifying, but at the same time, joyful.

This was necessary, I could hear myself saying again and again in my head. This was how I could get a scoop for Kirikiri Basara that even the media couldn't get. I'd get more hits. My name would spread all across the internet, and I'd have a ton more fans.

I imagined it, and I laughed again.

The bones were getting in the way, and the knife couldn't cut too deep. I tried plunging it in a little harder. The knife sliced right between the gap between the bones and ripped through the flesh as it dug deep, deep inside.

The professor wasn't moving, but his eyes were slick, shiny, wide-open, and staring right at me. Our eyes met.

Impulsively, I pulled the knife out from his body. I could hear him moan. I didn't want to hear it, so I stabbed the knife back into the same place I'd put it a minute ago. I pulled it out. Then I stabbed him again. And again. And again. And again. And again.

His chest was turning red with blood. My hands were turning crimson, too. And the whole time, I could see my face reflected in his eyes. I could see myself, laughing—

"No, that's not me!" I screamed. "I wasn't the last thing the professor saw before he died! I just happened to be there! I didn't do anything! When I found him, he was already dead! I wasn't the one who killed him—"

"There's no point in making excuses." I could hear a girl's husky voice in my ear.

And at the same time, the feeling of the floor beneath me vanished. My vision turned dark black, and the professor disappeared as well. I couldn't tell if I was floating or falling. I even thought I might be floating in the water. I reached out my hand, but there was nothing for me to grab. The only thing with me in the darkness was the girl's voice.

"You've got to live with a pain that's MUCH greater than death. That's your punishment, you understand?" Zonko appeared in the darkness before me, her tiny body floating amidst the black.

"I don't understand." I shook my head. "Help. Help me. Tell me this is all some kind of illusion..." Dr. Hashigami was dead. He'd been killed. Who did it? I had no clue. It wasn't me. I'd done nothing.

"Really?" As she floated, Zonko's cold voice stabbed into my brain stem. She was just a voice on the radio. How could she talk to me like that? "Are you sure you didn't kill him? Who could prove it?"

Prove it? I didn't know. But I didn't do it. I didn't do it!

"Sorry, but you..." Zonko floated right up to my nose and whispered, her expression unchanging. "You killed the professor in a horrible, brutal way."

When I woke up, I was lying facedown on my bed. The only things I could hear were the creak of bedsprings and rain outside the window.

I looked at the clock, and it was almost midnight. The room was dark. But it wasn't absolute darkness, like it had been before. Beyond the rain-slick windows I could see the darkness of the Kichijoji night, and the hazy lights of the buildings and streetlamps.

"A dream..." I sat up. My body felt heavy. I looked down and saw that I was still wearing my duffel coat. It was soaked with rain. That's right. When I'd come home, I'd fallen into bed without bothering to change.

As I tried to take it off, my hand slipped into my pocket. And there it was. A tiny, cold lump. I took it out fearfully. It was a gold tooth. It wasn't just a gold tooth, though. It was joined with a key.

I remembered the overwhelming stench of blood and felt like I wanted to throw up. My voice was a cross between a whisper and a moan. "Dr. Hashigami is dead."

It wasn't a dream, a hallucination, or anything else.

PARANORMAL SCIENCE NVL
Occultic;Nine
オカルティック・ナイン
THERE IS NO SUCH THING AS THE "OCCULT." IT CAN ALL BE DISPROVED BY SCIENCE.
ONLY THOSE WHO HAVE ACCEPTED EVERYTHING
HAVE THE RIGHT TO KNOW THE TRUTH.

▸ site 26: Shun Moritsuka —— 2/24 (Wednesday)

I felt like complaining to someone. Today, at long last, my patience had run out.

The darkness inside the university was torn apart by dozens of red lights. They looked blurry in the rain that had started a few hours ago.

I'd taken a look at what there was to see, and then come outside of Seimei University Building 10. I shivered from the cold rain. The courtyard in front of me was filled with police cars. By tomorrow morning, the grass where the students relaxed would be torn apart by tire tracks. I was surrounded by police officers, forensics people, and medical personnel that were rushing in and out of the building.

So, anyway. About why I was pissed off. I was pissed off because someone had committed a crime in the middle of the damn night. I wanted to tell every criminal in the entire world to knock this crap off. I wanted to yell and scream at them. Thanks to whoever did this, it was almost midnight when we cops arrived here. How come criminals never thought about *our* needs? It just wasn't fair.

But wait a second. This crime had happened hours before the

body was found. Forensics had told me that the estimated time of death was six to eight hours ago. That meant that if anyone was to blame, it wasn't the killer. It was whoever had discovered the body first.

"Christ! Whoever it was, I wish they would've thought about the time some more," I grumbled.

The body was discovered by a middle-aged security guard employed by the university. Supposedly, the reason that it had taken so long to find the body was that finals were over and the school was on spring break. Personally, I wished he could've held off a little longer and found it in the morning. Then I could've spent today working on rebuilding my *Vanguard* deck. *What if I end up losing to a middle school kid? What then?*

This really was a pain in the butt.

"Moritsuka."

I looked up and saw Kozaki and Shinoyama, two more detectives from the Musashino Police Department, jogging over to me. The looks on their faces told me that they'd been woken up from bed, and had hurriedly changed into their suits while their wives had complained to them. This work was tough on a married man.

"How was the scene?"

"Section 1 from the Tokyo Metro Police kicked me out halfway." I shrugged as I answered, and both of them looked up at the sky in exasperation. They'd completely lost any desire to go visit the crime scene.

"What's going on in there?" Asking that question was all they planned to do. I'd hoped that I could do the same thing, but I was unlucky enough to be the first detective from the Musashino Police

Station to arrive on the scene.

"The victim's name is Isayuki Hashigami, fifty-one years old. A professor at Seimei University's School of Science and Engineering." I smirked a little as I said the name, but neither Kozaki nor Shinoyama seemed impressed. "Huh? Did somebody already tell you the victim was Dr. Hashigami, the TV guy?"

"Yeah, I guess." Shinoyama nodded, and Kozaki looked down at my notebook.

"Moritsuka, your handwriting is shit."

"Hahaha... My mom tells me that a lot. I know it's lame."

"Can you even read that?"

"Of course. It's like shorthand, you know."

Both of them regarded me suspiciously. They didn't seem interested in it anymore, and motioned for me to continue talking.

"Um... The crime scene was his lab. It's on the sixth floor of Building 10 here. The estimated time of death is between 3:00 and 5:00 PM this afternoon." All the details would be shared when we put together a joint investigation task force later, so I decided just to give them the basic outline for now. "Um, the cause of death is... We're not sure at the moment."

"We don't need the 'um.'"

"Oh, sorry." I laughed and nodded. Shinoyama was the old, burly type of detective, and he loved to impress his ways on others. He could be a hassle to deal with. He was a talented detective, but for people from my generation, he was difficult.

"What do you mean, you're not sure?" Kozaki tilted his head. "Is that what forensics said?"

"There were wounds all over his body. He might've been tortured.

His legs look like they were bound, for one thing. And his trademark long hair was literally ripped off his scalp, or something."

Both of them wrinkled their brows in thought. Their detective's intuition told them that this might not be an ordinary killing.

"Was the murder weapon found?" Kozaki was still glancing at my notebook as he spoke.

"Oh, yeah. There was a bloody knife left at the scene. And in a really obvious place."

"An obvious place?"

"Yeah. Like the killer was trying to say, 'This is the murder weapon!'"

"Any fingerprints?"

"There were, I guess. Really clear ones, too. You can ask forensics for the details." They had to take the weapon back, get the fingerprints off it, and match them with the database. It would probably take them a while to figure out whose fingerprints they were. "Oh, and forensics was saying something else weird, too."

"Out with it."

"One of the victim's teeth had been removed, supposedly."

"One of his teeth?"

"It was one of those artificial teeth. Implants, they call 'em. Usually they're buried in pretty deep, so they're not supposed to be easy to remove. You'd need a pair of pliers or something to do it. And if you tried to rip one out, it would be so painful that the person would pass out."

"When was it taken out? Before or after his death?"

"We don't know. But we know it happened today."

"Hmm... Sounds pretty brutal."

"Makes it seem like the motive is a personal grudge, if you ask me."

"Anyway, it seems like us local police are supposed to go around and talk to witnesses." To be honest, I wasn't happy with the idea of going around questioning people in the middle of winter like this. The two of them must've agreed, because I could see a small look of disgust on their faces. "Oh, right. There's one more thing. This is a result of my personal investigations!"

"Your personal investigations?"

"Yes, you see, there's this particular doujinshi..."

"What's an, um... doujinshi?"

"Shinoyama, you don't know what a doujin is? Man, you're behind the times." I giggled a little, and Shinoyama's eyes narrowed. It felt like he was mad, so I decided to drop it. "A doujin is to manga as an indie band is to music."

"Manga doesn't have anything to do with this."

"You'd think so, right? But it does. Nobody else has noticed this yet, but when I heard about this case, I thought of it immediately. That's something that only an otaku could do. Heheheh."

"Did you find this doujin manga thing at the scene?"

"No, no. That's not it. This murder scene is almost identical to a scene from a certain doujinshi. That particular manga is an adult publication for women. Its author is a woman named Ririka Nishizono. Oh, if you need it, I can bring it to the station later. So in this manga, after this man's corpse gets raped, the rapist takes out his artificial tooth with a knife, as a memento, you see, and carries it home lovingly..."

"This is a waste of time."

"Moritsuka, what you just said is seriously creeping me out."

"Huh? Wha... Wait!" Shinoyama and Kozaki quickly ended the

conversation and entered Building 10. I was left alone in the rain.

"Sheesh. And I was nice enough to give them my big scoop, too," I muttered to myself. "Didn't they learn when they were kids that you should let people talk until they're finished? A detective's whole *job* is supposed to be listening to people."

Well, maybe it made sense that they wouldn't take me seriously. After all, I was a loser otaku who took his anime more seriously than his work. Ahaha. Anyway, I guess that meant my work was done for the day. I could let the elite detectives of the Tokyo Metropolitan Police, as well as my coworkers, handle this, and go home. Oh, but first I had to make a call.

I took out my phone and dialed the usual number. They picked up after the first ring. They must've been waiting for me to call.

"Agent Moritsuka," I said, in my very best English.

"You can speak Japanese."

"I'm Agent Moritsuka!"

"Are these EM waves secure?"

"Don't underestimate an otaku. This line is perfectly scrambled. No one can break this perfect algorithm."

They must've felt a little better after hearing that, because the voice on the phone chuckled a bit. "What's the situation?"

"The rain's pissing me off. I should've made a teru-teru bozu."

"The weather report says it will stop by tomorrow." I was joking, but they took me seriously. "Did you get the list?"

"No. I couldn't find the thing itself. But..."

"But?"

"I did find something."

"What do you mean?"

"The list we've been seeking for so long may not actually exist."

"What do you mean—"

"Code." I interrupted them midsentence. I could hear them gasp. "He had it written out in a damn dying message, of all things."

"That's bad."

"Of course, it's not a problem. I erased it before they saw it. I'm just glad I was the first one at the scene."

"I see."

"They haven't realized that the list they want to get rid of so badly has been coded."

"Does the list exist?"

"Yeah. But they went to the trouble of encoding and camouflaging it. I don't think it exists in paper form at all anymore. The professor's not that stupid."

"There's no time. Find the list."

"Time, huh? You mean the time limit of life? Still...there's too many of them to be just guinea pigs, right? I mean, 256 people?" I stopped and looked up through the rain at Seimei University Building 10. "But in the end..."

The voice on the phone fell silent. After a moment, the call ended.

"You probably can't change the future." My words melted into the cold rain.

site 27: MMG

The room was deep in the back of a long, long hallway in a subbasement, a place where even people who were allowed to be there rarely went. In that windowless room, the men were sitting once more in a circle. The man across from them, the only one in the room who was standing, was wearing his usual dark crimson suit.

"Why were the police called?" Dr. Matoba, in his white lab coat, asked angrily. "Takasu, don't you think that you were far too careless in this matter?"

Takasu, the man in the dark crimson suit, said nothing. Matoba tried to question him further, but Representative Hatoyama, who was sitting at his side, motioned for him to stop.

"There's no need to worry about the police. I had a little chat with him."

"But Mr. Hatoyama..."

"What's more important is the fact that the list still hasn't been found. What's going on with that?" His voice was as calm as it was when he spoke at the Diet, but his eyes weren't smiling at all.

Matoba interrupted before Takasu could answer. "You weren't able to learn anything from that nuisance Dr. Hashigami, were you?"

"Correct. The professor didn't say a word."

"And in the end, you killed him. How could you be so careless? Don't tell me it was just a simple mistake. I want explanations, and I want good ones—"

"There's a chance that the list may no longer exist on paper or as data." Takasu cut him off. "We 'investigated' Dr. Hashigami's house, but we couldn't find the list." Everyone here understood instantly that the 'investigation' he referred to was an illegal one. But, of course, no one pointed that out.

"However..." Takasu turned around and took a document off a serving cart next to him. He held it up at head height so that everyone could see. "There was a single locked drawer in the professor's desk. Inside, we found something interesting."

The men eagerly waited for him to say he'd found the list, but he silently shook his head. "Unfortunately, it's not the list. It's a draft for an article he was writing for a certain magazine."

"What of it? That sort of minor detail isn't what we're interested in."

"Let me finish, Mr. Hatoyama. The title of this draft is something of extreme interest to us."

"Extreme interest? You're certainly building this up, aren't you?"

"Hahaha, that wasn't my intent. The title is...'Time and the Spiritualizing World.'"

But even after Takasu's big reveal, the reaction of the listeners was less than positive. They were quiet, brows furrowed in confusion. The whole room was as silent and still as the surface of a placid lake.

What broke the silence wasn't the men sitting. It was a voice from a dark room that was sealed off by curtains. "'Spiritualizing,' you said?" When they heard the flat, emotionless voice, all the sitting men froze in surprise. No one—Takasu excepted—expected the speaker to be here, let alone intervene in the discussion. "And you're telling me that this is a clue to escaping the Prison of Time?"

Takasu turned towards the speaker. "Yes, most likely. I've already gathered RIKEN's primary members and am preparing for clinical trials with the information we've gained."

"The key to the prison, huh? Heheh..." There were no more words from behind the curtain.

"Eternal Life for the Bavarian Illuminati!"

"Eternal Life for the Bavarian Illuminati!"

Takasu spoke first and the men repeated after him, bowing their heads low.

PARANORMAL SCIENCE NVL
Occultic;Nine
オカルティック・ナイン
THERE IS NO SUCH THING AS THE "OCCULT." IT CAN ALL BE DISPROVED BY SCIENCE.
ONLY THOSE WHO HAVE ACCEPTED EVERYTHING
HAVE THE RIGHT TO KNOW THE TRUTH.

▸ site 28: Aria Kurenaino ——— 2/25 (Thursday)

The papers, the TV, and the internet had talked about nothing but the death of Dr. Isayuki Hashigami the whole day. According to the news, last night at around 11:00 PM, his body had been found covered in blood on the campus of Seimei University. Several hours ago, witnesses had seen a man fleeing from the scene, and the police were continuing their investigation.

And...

The biggest shock to me...

"His scalp had been torn off." Dr. Hashigami's trademark long hair had been ripped from his skull, scalp and all, and taken from the scene.

The talk shows on TV had been spending most of their time on this subject in particular. They'd played footage of Dr. Hashigami while he was still alive, while commentators with solemn expressions traded theories about the killer despite the fact that they had no evidence at all.

The debate on the net was more chaotic, with theories ranging from dark conspiracies to random spree killers. People claiming to be students at Seimei appeared on the boards and traded unverifiable gossip about Dr. Hashigami and his rivalries with other professors. It was like someone had poked a beehive.

Why did people enjoy discussing such vulgar things? Just looking at it all made me want to throw up, especially since Dr. Hashigami's death was something special to me. In my mind, I wondered if it was "my devil" that had killed Dr. Hashigami.

"The Devil's Ritual..." But my work at the black magic agency never included killing the target. I'd never told my devil to kill someone. I'd never done anything that would cause the target to die...right? I wasn't sure, and I shuddered.

How much did I know about my devil? All I ever did was sit in my shop and wait for him to talk to me. I'd never seen for myself what he did, and I'd never looked to see what became of the targets.

I thought back to the day I met my devil. I'd met that cruel, gentle devil as I'd stood at the brink of despair.

Three years ago, the most important person in the world to me had died due to medical malpractice at a hospital. There was no way my mind could handle that. Believing my brother was still alive, I secretly took his body from the hospital room and lived with it for a year. But my relatives had found out and shattered my happy illusion. My brother wasn't the handsome, gentle man who loved me anymore. He was a stinking, dried-up corpse. And when I'd been forced to face this, I ran.

As the despair tore into me, I found myself wandering through the streets of the neighborhood at night. I couldn't remember where I'd walked. Everything around me melted into the darkness, and I couldn't tell where I was. It hurt to breathe. I thought that perhaps I'd lost control of my lungs. I even thought of tearing open a hole in my throat to make it easier to breathe. I wasn't wearing shoes, so my toes had gone numb from the cold. My socks had torn, and my exposed toes were bleeding. There was no one there to help me. And even if there was, I didn't want help from anyone but my brother.

—I just wanted to disappear. I wanted to go to where my brother was. That was the only thing I thought. My brother was already gone from this world. I'd killed him twice, and now I'd been forced to confront that. There was no reason for me to live anymore.

Instead, I realized that if I died here, then maybe I could go be with my brother. And when I realized that, I felt a lot better.

So when I heard the sound, I was overjoyed to think that God had granted my request. It was the loud, rhythmic sound of a warning bell. Just listening to it made me feel uneasy.

In the darkness of the night, I could see two red lights flashing. It was a small train crossing. There were no people or cars nearby. On the other side of the lowered guardrails, I could see two sets of tracks. I could hear the sound of a train in the distance.

Instinctively, I put my hand on the guardrail. I told myself that all I had to do was go under it. On the other side, I'd find my brother.

At the time, I'd really felt like I'd been saved. I was excited. I was twitching with joy. My heart felt like it was going to burst. I wanted to shout with excitement.

I can still remember it now. I could see the lights of the train in the distance. I started to hear the sound of the warning bells, the beating of my heart, and the sound of the train on the tracks, all in slow motion.

It was time to end my life.

But just when I ducked down to go under the bar...

〈You have no right to that yet.〉

The voice felt like it came from a long way away, but it also seemed very close. It was hard to tell where it was coming from, but I suddenly gasped and forgot about going under the guard bar. Instead, I looked back behind me. There was no one there.

"Brother?! Is that you, Brother?!" My voice was drowned out by the roar of the yellow train as it passed by an instant later. But even next to the noisy train, I could hear every word the voice said, as if it were directly inside my head.

〈Death is something that's given to the chosen. And you still ain't got that right.〉

"It's you, isn't it, Brother?! Where are you?! Please, let me see you!" I shouted to make myself heard over the passing train.

〈Nope. I ain't your brother. So don't go thinking I am.〉 The voice was a man's low, unpleasant whisper.

This wasn't my brother's voice. My brother's voice wasn't ugly like this. The two voices were nothing alike. This voice was something more terrifying. When I realized that, my whole body started to get goosebumps. At some point, I'd begun to shake.

The train passed, and the warning bells stopped. The guardrail slowly rose. All that was left was the silence and darkness.

But I couldn't move a step away. "I'm hearing things again, aren't I?" That's what I tried to tell myself. Just like I'd imagined the voice of my brother when he was already a mummy, now I was imagining the voice of a different man, one I'd never met. I was insane, so it was certainly possible.

〈This ain't a hallucination.〉 The voice wouldn't let me escape from reality that easily. 〈Don't try to make me out to be a part of you. I'm my own creature.〉

I was talking with it. The cold wind blew through my hair. It felt like someone was breathing onto the nape of my neck, and I held myself tight.

"Then...you're..."

In my mind, I repeated to myself what the voice had just said. *Death is something that's given to the chosen.* Then the speaker was—

As someone who knew about black magic, there was one possibility that came to mind. "You're a devil, aren't you?"

〈...〉

"You're a devil, right?"

〈Yeah, that's right,〉 the voice answered.

"Heheh...heheheh... I knew it. You're my devil. My own, personal devil..." I realized that this was my punishment for my sins. I wasn't going to be allowed to die. I wasn't going to be allowed to see my brother again. This was the fate of an insane little sister who'd defiled her brother's body. I would be forced to suffer that pain until being chosen gave me the "right" to die, and only then could I see my brother again.

That's why I had decided not to die. No, more precisely, in that moment, at that crossing, the girl named Ria Minase died at the hands of that devil, and I was reborn as Aria Kurenaino. Ever since then, it had been my devil that kept me alive. He wasn't my master, nor I his. Perhaps it was better to say that we were only bound by a contract. That's why we didn't interact more than necessary.

For the past two years, I'd never even thought about what the devil was doing when it wasn't with me. Was it possible for "my devil" to actually kill anyone?

I left my home earlier than usual and walked through the rain to the House of Crimson. When I got there, it felt colder than usual, and I was astonished.

I felt a presence.

"You're here, aren't you?" I asked, fearfully.

〈Yup.〉

I hadn't expected the devil to be waiting for me. That had never happened before. And now of all times, too. Perhaps it had read my mind and realized my doubts. Or had it decided to test me, on a whim? To see whether I was worthy of making a contract with it. If I got a single answer wrong, the devil would show me no mercy.

I took off my coat and started to think about what to do.

〈You know Isayuki Hashigami's dead?〉

I almost shouted in surprise. I hadn't expected the devil to bring it up, either. It felt like even if I lied, he'd be able to tell from the way I moved and acted that I wasn't telling the truth. So I sat down in my usual spot in the shop and decided to tell him the truth.

"Did you do that?"

〈Hmph. That ain't funny.〉 The demon's dry chuckle echoed in my mind.

It was enough to make me shiver. "Really?"

〈What, did you think I did it? Did it scare you so much you pissed your pants?〉

"The contract we made said that you wouldn't kill anyone."

〈The contract said I wouldn't tell you what I did.〉

There was no way I could out-argue a devil. I was even afraid I might anger it. This wasn't someone I could open up to.

I could hear the devil click his tongue in aggravation. 〈Don't you go freaking out on me. Lately, you'd finally started to get a hold of your damn self. Are you going back to who you used to be? 'Cause if you piss me off too much—〉 The devil suddenly fell silent.

"What's wrong?"

There was no answer. Only the silence lingered.

I wondered where he'd gone, but I could still sense his presence in the shop. I squeezed Ahriman's head—that was the doll I was holding—and held my breath.

Suddenly the bulb from the antique light stand exploded with a loud burst.

"Eeyah!" I quickly moved to shield my face with Ahriman. I looked and saw tiny fragments of broken light bulb glass on the floor.

This was the power of "my devil." This was the first time I'd seen it for myself. All he'd ever done before was talk to me.

For the first time, I saw his power, and the terror was enough that I could barely move. I couldn't stand up from my chair. Had I gone in too deep? But the devil...

〈I hadn't done anything to him yet,〉 he said. 〈I was willing to do it, but someone got to him ahead of me. Something doesn't feel right about all this. If somebody's trying to set me up...then I have to figure out what I'm going to do about that.〉 The devil's voice was filled with anger.

His anger wasn't directed towards me. It was directed at some unseen power that even a devil hadn't been able to predict. Perhaps the two of us had gotten involved in something very complicated. If I'd known this was going to happen, perhaps I would've been more careful when a bloody ball of hair showed up in my mailbox.

〈You're gonna help me, too. If you refuse, the next thing that explodes is gonna be your head. Got it?〉

I glanced at the shattered light stand, licked my dry lips, and slowly nodded. "I understand. No one can be allowed to find out about your existence, after all."

You couldn't trust a devil, but I couldn't afford to lose my partner. I wasn't going to let anyone else have him. Until he gave me the death I longed for—

▸ site 29: Toko Sumikaze ——— 2/25 (Thursday)

The *Mumuu* editorial department was a little more on edge than usual. The news had said this morning that Dr. Hashigami had been killed, and our department had gotten several calls. Most of them had been from the media. None of the editors even knew what was really going on with the case. After all, I was his editor, and I still couldn't believe it had happened.

"Sumikaze!" Takafuji, our editor-in-chief, came over to my desk looking angry. "Did you get in touch with Dr. Hashigami's family yet?"

"No, not yet..." I'd tried calling several times already, after the first time he'd asked.

I'd worked with the professor for almost a year, but I'd actually only met his family a few times. Almost all of my meetings had been with him alone.

"I guess we can't show up at his house at a time like this, can we?" The editor-in-chief looked like he wasn't sure what to do.

I remembered that I'd been there a few times before. I actually didn't really like going. There were...*things*...in that house. I had a pretty strong sixth sense, and I was sensitive to that stuff, so I could tell. I'd felt a strong presence in that house, one with an extremely rare strength.

But that didn't matter right now.

"What are we supposed to tell his family, anyway?" I asked. "Are we supposed to ask what to do with the money we hadn't paid him yet? That's way too insensitive."

"Then maybe while we're at the wake..."

"The wake isn't happening yet," I sighed.

"Oh, that's right! The wake! Maybe we can talk to his wife then. Or his mom."

"I'm not sure... That might not be the right time, I think."

Takafuji scratched his head. "Fine. At least find out when the wake is, and when you know, send flowers. We can put off all the details until later."

"Um, sir..." I ran after him before he could get back to his desk, but then I hesitated a moment before I brought it up. "We're...canceling his column, right?"

"Did you get this month's draft already?"

"No, not yet..."

"Then we don't have a choice, do we? It's not like we can have a ghost writing for our magazine."

"The thing is, he'd said he wanted to start writing about a new theme. His first draft was already completed, he said."

The editor-in-chief shrugged. I couldn't read his expression. "When was this?"

"Last month." I could've gotten the draft then, but it was too late for regrets now.

"His last work, huh? If that's true, I want to have it." But before I could agree, he put his hand on my shoulder. "For now, think up another article for us to run."

"What?! R-right now?!"

"Right now! Sorry, but do it!" That was all he said before he left the office. There was no chance to argue with him. He was just going to make me do all the work.

"Ascension," I went back to my seat and sighed. I wasn't feeling as shocked as I'd thought I would.

Dr. Hashigami had always been very friendly to me during our meetings, even though I was still a newbie editor. So when I'd heard he'd been killed, my whole mind had gone blank. But there'd been much to do after that, and I found myself going about my business as normal. Would I feel sadder if I went to the funeral and saw the body?

Who could've killed him, anyway? Did the police have any idea? Why would anyone want to do it?

"I guess there's no point in thinking about it." I decided to start by organizing Dr. Hashigami's drafts. If I was doing something, it would stop me from thinking about things.

My policy was to always keep things clean. In a room full of messy editors' desks, mine was the only one that was organized. I kept all of Dr. Hashigami's columns in a single file. But there were also the notes I'd taken during my meetings with him, and the books he'd given me to read. The books, especially, I would have to return to the family. I wanted to get everything organized now so that I wouldn't have to rush when I needed them.

Dr. Hashigami was a university professor, and he loved to teach people things. Every time we met so he could give me his draft, he'd also give me a couple of books he'd found interesting. By now, I had almost twenty of the things. I'd been working my way through them, but I was busy with my work as an editor and didn't have as much time to read as I wanted.

All the books were still in a paper bag under my desk. *Professor, I'm sorry...*I apologized in my mind as I took them out. It felt like I should read as many of them as I could before I gave them back. I took them all out of the bag so that I could see what they were.

"Oh..." Mixed in with the pile of books was the notebook I thought I'd lost a month ago.

It was a small B6 notebook, about five by seven inches, with a brown cover. I'd gone for function over form, so it wasn't especially cute. That was definitely mine. I'd almost given up on finding it. *How did it get in here?*

I was glad that I'd found it now, I thought. This was the notebook I'd used during many of my meetings with Dr. Hashigami. Perhaps Dr. Hashigami's soul had done me one last little kindness before heading off into the next world. Or was that inappropriate to think?

I flipped through the pages to see what was inside. Looking back over it now, I could see that it was filled with words I didn't know. But every word I saw reminded me of what Dr. Hashigami was talking about when I wrote it.

"Huh?" Suddenly my vision blurred. I'd started crying, somehow. Was I finally starting to feel sad?

I took off my glasses and wiped the corners of my eyes. I needed to make sure I went to the wake and the funeral. I needed to say goodbye. And if he did write one last article, I wanted to make sure the world saw it. Of course, I'd need to get his family's permission.

"Hmm?" As I flipped through the pages, lost in thought, one part caught my attention. It was written in red pen, as opposed to black or blue, and marked "important" as well.

There were three phrases there: "the bottom of the water," "moonlight," and "many people."

"What was this, again?" It was definitely my handwriting. I could vaguely remember writing it. But I couldn't remember what we were talking about, or what it meant. "Hmm... I'm pretty sure it was sometime recent, too." Probably last month, when I'd met him.

I tried to remember, but I couldn't. I could remember everything else in the notebook, but this one critical part had faded from my mind. It was really starting to bother me.

"I should calm down." *Maybe I should go to the convenience store and get a coffee or something.*

I closed the notebook and put it on the desk, then sat up. I left the editorial office and headed for the elevators. Just as I pressed the button to go down, a light shock, like static electricity, went through my fingers. And at the same time, images came flooding into my head.

"Ascension!" I screamed. I looked around, and was relieved to see that there was no one there. "I remember! I remember!"

When the static electricity had hit me, I'd remembered what had happened when I'd written those words. It was last month, when I'd gone to get Dr. Hashigami's article draft and had a brief chat with him about his future plans. He'd asked me a question, which was unusual for him.

—Sumikaze, do you remember any of your dreams lately? If any words come to mind immediately, I'd like you to tell them to me.

And that's when I'd told him "the bottom of the water," "moonlight," and "many people." I didn't really remember the dreams themselves. Dreams always fade from your mind so quickly. But I remembered writing those words down.

"Why did he ask me that? Was he planning on writing about dreams?" In the end, I'd never know.

"Dr. Hashigami was murdered."

▸ site 30: Miyuu Aikawa ———— 2/26 (Friday)

"Huh? You're going back to that weird café?"

Chi looked shocked. I'd been cleaning the classroom with her after school and talking about my plans for the day. I nodded as I swept the floor with a broom.

"Which means you're meeting that weird older boy again?"

She was talking about Gamo. When he'd come to the AV room before, she'd been there too, of course. And of course, she'd seen me talk to him. I remembered her asking me a bunch of questions about that later.

"He's strange, but he's not...*weird,* you know?" If anybody there was weird, it was Master Izumin. He was pretty bizarre.

"I don't know... I mean, he runs one of those shady websites, right? I saw it. He was saying all this stuff about you."

"Myu?! Chi, you saw that?" I really didn't want any of my real-world friends seeing that, maybe. Gamo was really making a big deal out of things online.

"Hey, Myu, are you sure about this? You can be a bit of an airhead, so I'm worried."

"An airhead... Nobody but you has ever said that to me."

"You are. I mean, you remember that one writer with the occult magazine who wanted to interview you?"

"You mean Toko from *Mumuu*?"

"That's right. She did the interview, but never wrote the article, right?"

I'd met Toko Sumikaze several months ago. Back when our livestream was still more or less unknown, Toko had happened to see it by chance. She'd contacted me and said she wanted to write about me in *Mumuu*.

"They ran out of space, is all. And she apologized later." In the end, she'd had to scrap the article, but she and I had really gotten along well, and once in a while, we still sent messages to one another.

"That person with *Mumuu* might have turned out to be a good person, but there's lots of people who aren't. If you ever think you're in danger, even a little, let me know, okay?" Her hands were folded together, and she was panting a little. She was really worried about me.

"Umyu...I'm so happy you're my friend." I jumped and grabbed her, and she rubbed my head.

"There, there. I'll protect you, my little airheaded Myu."

"Okay, then buy me a cream chocolate banana crepe at Circus."

"Don't get cocky." She poked me slightly on the head.

"Hey, you girls, get to work!" The other boys who were cleaning the classroom complained, and we quickly got back to work.

All the after-school clubs had been canceled since yesterday. I was pretty sure it was because they still hadn't caught the murderer responsible for the death that took place at the university campus next door. When the homeroom teacher had told us to make sure we were home before dark, some of the boys in the class had complained. "We're not in elementary school," they'd said.

When I finished cleaning, I left the school with Chi. We walked the path lined with gingko trees to the station. In fall, this path was covered with yellow leaves, but by now they were long gone, and it felt pretty lonely.

It was a pretty long walk from the school to Kichijoji Station, about twenty minutes or so. There was a bus stop in front of the school, but the bus was always super crowded, and both Chi and I avoided it as much as we could.

"You told my fortune once before, didn't you?"

"Yeah. It was about two or three months ago, wasn't it? I saw a little birdie, didn't I?" But Chi didn't own a bird, and neither she nor her family had anything to do with them. We never really figured out what it meant.

"Ever since you saw it, I've been thinking about birds. I started looking at pictures of birds on the internet, and found one I wanted."

"Yeah? What kind of bird?"

"A parakeet."

"Wow, that's great! Then maybe what I saw was the parakeet you're going to get."

"Ahaha... I hope so. I'm trying to persuade my mom to let me get it. Here, take a look." She showed me a photo she'd taken on her cell phone.

It was a picture of a parakeet with brilliant lemon-colored plumage. She must've taken it while she was moving, because it was a little blurry.

"It's so cute! But you're a bad photographer, Chi."

"Don't say that." Whenever she took a picture, it was always blurry. It had happened a bunch of times before.

"Where did you take this picture? Is it real?"

"There's a pet shop near my house. That's where I found it. I go at least once every three days lately. I'm just looking, so it doesn't bother the shop."

Once every three days was a lot. She was really dedicated. She must have really wanted it.

"How much is a parakeet, anyway?"

"He's five thousand yen."

"That's a lot, huh? You couldn't buy it with your allowance."

"You need to get a cage and stuff, too, so it's actually a lot more than that." Five thousand yen was a ton of money for a student. High school girls in particular spent a lot of money all the time.

"I hope you can persuade your mom."

"Yeah. If I get it, I've already picked a name. I'm gonna call it Dodo."

"Huh? What's that mean? It's kind of...weird."

"I figured you wouldn't know what it's from. It's from *Alice in Wonderland*. The Dodo. That's where I got the name."

That was just like Chi, maybe. She loved fairy tales and children's stories, and she always said her dream was to write children's books.

"Was the Dodo in *Alice* a parakeet, though?"

"It wasn't, but that doesn't matter!" I'd thought she'd put a lot of effort into it, but maybe she hadn't given it that much thought after all.

"Chi, you're gonna regret that. I mean, Dodo? Isn't that a lame name? Let's think of something else." I tried my best to persuade her, but she pouted.

"...I'll think about it. I still don't know if I'll be able to get one, anyway. I'm stopping on the way home today, too, though." We were having so much fun talking that it felt like we got to the station in a flash.

"Okay, see you later. Bye!" We waved and said goodbye in front of the station.

I went to Blue Moon on my own after that, but neither Gamo nor Narusawa were there, and I ended up having to spend an hour or so talking to Master Izumin. By the time I staggered home, exhausted, the sun had already set.

I looked down at my phone as I changed out of my uniform and saw a message from Chi. "Birdie ba" was all it said. There was a weird photo attached.

"Chi, your picture's blurry again." It was so blurry I couldn't tell where it was taken. All I could tell was that it was taken on a street somewhere. There was a single trading card lying on the ground. The sun was setting. There was a long shadow that probably belonged to her. It felt, though, like nobody who saw the picture would pay any attention to those things.

There was something big in the top right, something really strange. That's what they'd notice instead. It was like a ray of white light and was clearly different than the rest of the scenery surrounding it. It wasn't a natural light. I'd seen pictures like this before on TV when I was a little girl.

"A ghost picture?" I hurriedly sent Chi back a message asking what this was. I called her, too. But she didn't answer my message, and she didn't pick up the phone.

Saturday and Sunday were the weekend, but on Monday, the next day of school, Chi wasn't there.

PARANORMAL SCIENCE NVL
Occultic;Nine
オカルティック・ナイン
THERE IS NO SUCH THING AS THE "OCCULT." IT CAN ALL BE DISPROVED BY SCIENCE.
ONLY THOSE WHO HAVE ACCEPTED EVERYTHING
HAVE THE RIGHT TO KNOW THE TRUTH.

▸ site 31: MMG

"What's the status of the bugs with the first generation?"

There was no inflection in Takasu's voice as he answered Hatoyama's question. "As I've said in my previous reports, the electronic capabilities of the first generation continue to increase as a result of the experiments. Their affinity with the spirit world is growing stronger than anticipated. The increase in bug factors is an effect of that."

"My question is how you're dealing with the problem."

For once, Hatoyama's question was met with silence. But Takasu's expression didn't change, and Hatoyama seemed a bit impatient.

He continued. "Is it possible, for example, to adjust the output of 'Odd Eye,' and expand our control radius to deal with the bugs? That thing was Nikola Tesla's greatest invention, after all. And its capabilities have grown far, far beyond the 1932 Wardenclyffe Tower, yes?"

"You're correct, but the precise adjustments required would be difficult. Too low, and we can't get data for our experiments. Too high, and the affinity will only grow stronger. Its current setting is the greatest we can use to allow it to interfere with the guinea pigs."

"But that doesn't mean it's a good idea to ignore the bug factors," Dr. Matoba interrupted, bitterly. "What happens if we continue the experiment?"

"There's a possibility that the guinea pigs which we had some degree of control over will grow more and more feral."

The seated men responded to Takasu's statement with disappointment and disillusionment.

"Just sitting back and watching won't improve the situation." Hatoyama's shoulders slumped as he spoke.

"If we act now, we can be a little forceful and still not have any issues. That's the purpose of the 'occult,' after all."

Matoba agreed. "We've used all available forms of media to create that fad, all in preparation for this. This country is in the midst of the biggest occult boom in twenty years. All you have to do is turn on the TV, and morning and night the news will be showing features on ghost photographs."

"Controlling the populace is normally a difficult proposition, but in the sole sense of distancing them from the spirit world, we've succeeded thanks to the power of the occult," Hatoyama said. He, Matoba, and the other seated men all looked satisfied.

"Takasu, come up with a method to deal with the 256 people in the first generation. This is your responsibility."

Takasu's eyes narrowed at Hatoyama's orders, but he slowly nodded. "Understood. Leave it to me."

▸ site 32: Ririka Nishizono ——— 2/29 (Monday)

I softly folded up my blue umbrella. Just as I did, a raindrop blew down from the tree above me and landed right on my head. The coldness made me shiver. I just barely managed to avoid gasping out loud.

It was afternoon on a weekday in the middle of winter, and Inokashira Park was usually empty at this time. With the rain having just come to an end, there was barely anyone here. That's why I always found myself coming here whenever it rained. I'd walk through the silent park with my blue umbrella. It was enough to make myself imagine I was in a fantasy world, and it made me very happy.

And today, I'd found something unexpected, as well.

"A devil haunts this park!" The man was on the park's open-air stage, giving a speech. It was more like screaming than a speech, though.

I was his only audience. I certainly didn't expect to meet him here. I must have used up all my good luck for the day. I'd seen people talking about him before online.

—In Inokashira Park, you can find God.

"God" was him.

He was wearing a filthy blouse jacket, sweatpants, and a white baseball cap with vertical stripes that was stained black in places. The shoulders of his blouse jacket were covered with dandruff. He was short and hunched over. There was no way to tell how old he was, but his face was lined with wrinkles. He had to be at least fifty.

"The land of Musashino is tainted with the electromagnetic rays of Wardenclyffe! Of course, this park is tainted, too!" God's voice echoed clearly throughout the quiet park.

The only people in this space now were me and God. It seemed to me a very happy encounter. And for some reason...what he said seemed strangely interesting. So I simply stood there in silence, and tried my best to make out what he was saying through the screams and shouts.

"Nikola Telsa's experiment continues! It's a worldwide system using the Tokyo EM towers!"

What did he think of my presence here? He hadn't looked at me once since I'd stopped here to listen to him. There was no way he wouldn't have noticed me. From up on the outdoor stage, he could see his surroundings clearly.

So why didn't he try to look at me? Did he not care about me? Was he so caught up in his own words that he didn't care about anyone else? Was he too drunk to realize that there were other people around? Was he deliberately ignoring me? Was he simply embarrassed? Could God get embarrassed? No matter how old he was, it hurt my feminine pride a little to be completely ignored by a man.

Of course, he had no idea what I was thinking. He just kept yelling.

Once in a while, he would bring the bottle of sake he was holding up to his mouth, but it was already empty. But after a while, he would forget that it was empty, and bring it back up to his lips, only to get angry when he found it was empty. Then a bit later, the process would repeat.

"How cute..." I whispered so he wouldn't hear me.

It was a personal theory of mine that every man in the world was cute. Their age didn't matter. I felt myself becoming unable to hold back. I wanted to capture his every moment and put it down on paper. I thought that impulses like that only existed in manga.

I decided to sit down on a bench in front of the stage. But the bench was wet from the rain, and if I did sit down, I'd get covered in mud. I didn't want to do that, but I quickly got an idea, and put the weekly manga magazine I'd bought this morning down on the bench. Then I sat down on it. Now I wouldn't have to worry about getting wet. I felt a little bad for the model on the cover of the magazine, but I was very pleased with myself for coming up with the idea.

As I sat down, I could hear a clink from the pendant on my chest. I'd bought the pendant on impulse because I liked the sound. But God didn't even seem interested in the sound.

"Two huge antennas are pointed at Musashino twenty-four hours a day, right under the public's eyes! The fact that the people don't show their rage is proof that they're brainwashed!"

—I knew he noticed me, too.

Just imagining it made the filthy old man seem even cuter, and I shivered. I took out my sketchbook from my bag, and carefully observed him as I ran my pencil down the white page. I would sketch a portrait of God. The idea struck me as romantic, and I chuckled to myself. Perhaps I would make it the title of my next book.

"You can't see it, hear it, or smell it! But it eats away at our lives! The hospitals won't help! They're full of dark conspiracies!"

God was a worthy model for a sketch. There was an incredible intensity in his wrinkled face, and in the way the saliva flew from his mouth as he spoke. It would've been nice if he could've stood still while he maintained that expression, but I couldn't exactly give God posing instructions. That wasn't the only reason it wasn't turning out the way I wanted. My hands were also turning numb from the cold.

I'd started drawing this sketch on a whim. Should I continue it? Or should I stop? I was uncertain, but I kept drawing, when—

I heard footsteps on the gravel behind me. I felt like someone had interrupted my private time with God. I resisted the urge to sigh and turned around.

There was a small young man standing there, in a brown suit, a beige trench coat, and a beige cap. "Huh? That's strange. The guy on Yahoo Auctions told me that this was where he'd hand over the *Vanguard* card. Maybe it was a mistake to believe someone who wanted to hand it over in person." He was tilting his head and saying something I really didn't understand.

My holy encounter came to an end, and the stadium quickly returned to the vulgar, normal world. The young man kept looking around, and then fixed his gaze on me.

"Oh, are you the person I'm supposed to be trading with? My screen name is 'Hello there, I'm Zenigata.'"

"I don't know what you're talking about. I'm sorry," I said with a smile.

The young man took off his cap and slowly bowed. "My apologies.

You see, I won an auction for a rare *Vanguard* card. I picked one where I could get the card in person so that I could show it off to those bratty middle schoolers as soon as possible, and they told me to meet them here. But it looks like I've been tricked. Man, what a screw-up. But you know, there are a lot of very pretty women like you who play *Vanguard* lately, so I did have some small hope in my heart when I spoke to you, you see."

He was squirming a little as he moved. How strange. At least, there was no one I knew who was like him.

"Heh...what a cute student you are. Is that cosplay?"

"I may not look it, but I'm a college graduate. This is my work uniform."

"Oh? Then you're older than me. Still, if you ask me, you're very cute."

The man in the trench coat with the boyish face suddenly assumed a very serious expression and stood straight up. "You've just stolen something very important from me."

"Oh? What might that be? What is it that's so important?"

"My heart."

I'd heard that phrase somewhere before. I couldn't help but break out laughing. He had the line and the motion down pat, but he was still tiny, with a young boy's face, so it all looked so funny.

"By the way." He gestured towards the stage.

"The pollution is not limited to Musashino, nor to Tokyo, nor even to Japan! It's already spreading out into the whole world!" God was still shouting, oblivious to me and the boy in the trench coat.

"Who is that guy?"

"God."

He looked surprised at my answer. "You know God?"

"No. I don't know him."

"But you're drawing that old guy—I mean, God—"

"I'm just doing it on my own. I haven't spoken to him."

"He won't get mad?"

"He doesn't seem to care, actually. I'm sure God is a very tolerant person."

"May I see?" I nodded happily, and handed him my incomplete sketch. "Wow, this is great! Are you with one of the wall circles? Hmm... But wait. This isn't a moe type of picture, is it? It's very good, though. I think I've seen it somewhere before. Hmm, are you a student? Maybe at an art school?"

I shook my head. "I'm a student, but not at an art school. At Seimei over there."

"Do they have an art major over there?"

"They don't."

"Your drawing's too good for you to be a mere student..." He thought for a moment about something that didn't matter at all, and then suddenly raised his head in surprise. "That's right. This is Kichijoji. There are a lot of manga authors that live in Kichijoji. That means you must be a manga author, too! Let me shake your hand! And then I'll never wash it again!"

I hadn't said a word about being a manga author, but he offered his hand out to me anyway. I looked at it and shrugged.

"I am a manga author, but not a professional one."

"Does that mean you go to Comiket? What genre? If it's BL, that's kind of not my thing. But I really do think that I've seen this art style before."

I wasn't quite sure how to handle the way he was talking. It was as if he knew something and was playing dumb, waiting for me to say it myself. No, it wasn't "like" that at all. He was after me from the start. But he wasn't here to hit on me. He was here for some other reason. My intuition was sharp when it came to those things.

I decided to try and tease him a little.

"You're lying, aren't you?"

"What do you mean?" He tilted his head in surprise. Every movement he made was overly dramatic.

I sighed audibly. "Where did you see my books? I'd like to know. Tell me. That is, if this isn't some elaborate pickup attempt."

"Hmm... The thing is, I really can't remember. Man, I'm so lame. I'm really feeling lame right now. Sorry, can you at least tell me your pen name? Or even the name of one of your doujinshi. Maybe I've read it."

"My pen name is Ririka Nishizono, or—"

"Yes, I know that." He was the one who told me to give him my name, but before I could finish, he cut me off and grabbed my hand.

The look in his eyes had changed. It was like a sheep instantly transforming into a wolf. And that was what made the smile when he grabbed my hand so scary.

"I thought so. You knew it from the start, didn't you? You're very mean."

"Your book, *The Bottom of the Dark Water*, is being talked about a lot online. Did you know that?" He rubbed the palm of my hand as he spoke.

"Are you sure it's online?"

"Of course."

"Are they talking about how it's not very good, for instance?"

"Yes. I read it myself, and it wasn't." I much preferred to have him tell me that right to my face. Not that I would ever like him. "But it was very interesting. Particularly the third story. That was very good."

"The third story?" It was pornography about the twisted love between two men. "I thought you weren't into BL?"

"Correct. But the contents of the story were very interesting. I've been hoping I could get a chance to ask you how you came up with it. I mean, most people couldn't dream up a story like that. Who would ever think of raping your lover's corpse, then ripping out their tooth with a knife as a memento?"

It was the strangest thing imaginable to be talking about on an afternoon in a park after the rain, and I couldn't help but twist my lips in a chuckle. "I don't come up with my ideas." I softly shook his hand away.

I stood up from the bench and stared into his eyes. He didn't look away. Was he trying to find out what I was thinking? Or perhaps, trying to keep me from seeing what he was thinking?

"Offer up a sacrifice! Offer up a sacrifice before the world system is complete!" As we stared into each other's eyes, as if in an intense love scene, God ignored us and kept screaming.

I took a step back from him. "Everything I draw is—" I took back my sketchbook. "Something I see in my dreams."

And when I told him that, he suddenly sighed. "Anyway, about the code..."

I was uncertain how to handle this sudden change of subject. It was just like earlier. He wasn't letting me take control of the conversation.

"Did you say...cord? Like earphones?"

"No, no. C. O. D. E. *Code.*"

"I don't understand."

"If you're seeing things in your dreams and putting them into your manga, are those dreams prophetic ones?"

And now we were back to the same subject as before. I was getting all confused. The boy in the trench coat pulled a piece of paper out of his pocket and handed it to me.

"This is a copy of your work, *The Bottom of the Dark Water*." He pointed to a very ordinary panel. One of the objects in the background was circled in red pen. "Look here. There's letters written there, right? In the English alphabet. What do they say?"

"C, O, L, A." It was a bottle of soda. I'd modeled it after an image I found online. I'd fiddled with it a bit, though.

"No, that's not right. You can tell, can't you? You drew the thing."

"Yes. This says C, O, D, E. What of it?" Then he took out a photograph.

It was evidently taken in a dark room. On the floor, in red paint, I could just barely make out the word "code."

"Does this have something to do with my work?"

"It was the dying message of a murder victim."

My dream had become real.

"Who...*are* you?" I asked. I couldn't even hear God's speech anymore.

"You should know who I am without me needing to tell you. I may not look it, after all, but I'm—" He smiled a thin smile and drew closer to me, and whispered into my ear. "I'm the detective in your manga."

▸ site 33: Yuta Gamon ———— 2/29 (Monday)

Eyes, eyes, eyes...

Everyone was looking at me. That's how it felt.

A suspect in a brutal murder. A crazy man. A psychopath. A murderer. An inhuman piece of shit. That's what all their eyes seemed to say. I imagined it, and froze.

The rain had been falling all weekend, so I was able to hide my face with an umbrella, but today it had stopped. The sun had set and it was dark, but my heart was pounding fast.

"The keyhole... I have to find the keyhole..."

I was a fugitive.

The cops must have figured out who I was long ago. Even the news said so. They said someone had been seen fleeing from the scene of Dr. Hashigami's murder.

By now my photo must be all over the internet, and everybody on the streets must be frantically searching for me. There was no way of knowing when somebody would point me out. It could happen just a few seconds from now.

"The keyhole..." I suddenly saw a condo building that was under construction, and staggered towards it. The workers must have been off for the day, because it was empty.

There was a fence surrounding it, and an ordinary, worn padlock on it. The fence could be opened and closed like an accordion to make an entrance, and the padlock was locking it.

"The keyhole!" I staggered up to it and took the gold tooth key out of my pocket. I plunged it into the padlock's keyhole. "Fit... Come on, fit..."

Of course, it didn't fit at all.

"Why... Why won't it fit?" If I tried to force it, the gold tooth key might shatter or break. I had no choice but to give up and leave.

I kept walking around and looking for keyholes, trying my best to stay out of sight. This key was the one thing that could get me out of this mess. That's why I had no choice but to cling to it. In my head, I knew that I wasn't going to find the keyhole that easily. But if I wanted to save myself, I had no choice but to keep looking.

As I walked through the cold, I eventually found myself in front of the Hachiman Shrine. The street was packed with cars, and I could hear angry honking. It felt louder than usual. I carefully looked down the street and saw that the cause was in front of Anyoji Temple, right next to the Hachiman shrine.

It was crowded with people, and there were lights everywhere. I panicked when I realized that they were all with the media. I half-remembered hearing on the afternoon news that Dr. Hashigami's funeral was going to be held at Anyoji today.

From the sidewalk, I couldn't see the main building of the temple. To get inside the temple, you had to follow a little path and go through a gate. In front of the gate, I could see a bunch of reporters from different stations with their backs to the temple, talking into cameras with serious expressions on their faces. It was just about time for the evening news, so these were probably live broadcasts.

"Ah...ah..." I couldn't get any closer. There was no way. If I went inside the temple, they'd put me on TV. And what was I supposed to say to the professor's family? I couldn't tell them that I'd found his body, yanked out his tooth, and run away! There was no way I could let the media see me. The police had to have been leaking them information. They must know what I looked like.

I needed to get out of here. I turned around and headed up the way I'd come. I wasn't sure if I was shaking because of the cold, or something else. My hands were so numb that I couldn't even feel the pain.

I should just go home.

Don't let anyone find you. Don't let anyone suspect you. Don't look up. Just look down, and drag yourself home.

I felt so pathetic and guilty that I wanted to throw up.

"I'm practically...a *criminal*," I groaned.

Was I going to just drop out of society like this? I hadn't been to school since the day I'd found the professor's body. I looked so awful that Mom let me stay home without really saying anything. None of my classmates at school would've been worried about me. Ryotasu was the only one who'd called a few times, and I'd ignored her. At this rate, I'd turn into a real NEET who never left his room.

This wasn't how it was supposed to happen. This wasn't what I wanted.

Why did I go see Dr. Hashigami that day? I wanted to cry, but I didn't want the people around me to get suspicious, so I held it back.

The tension kept eating away at me. I felt heavy. Just walking was exhausting. The sheer number of cars and people around me was making it hard to breathe.

I couldn't take it anymore, so I headed down a narrow alleyway. Once you went down an alley around here, you'd find yourself in the residential area that ran along Itsukaichi Street. It was a lot less crowded.

"Keyhole..." I passed in front of an abandoned house. The glass in the front door was cracked. It must have been abandoned a long time. I moved up against the door in the darkness, fumbled for the keyhole, and then pushed the key in.

"Fit...Fit!" I forced the key into the keyhole, snot dripping down my nose. And then I remembered...

Shouldn't I give this key—this *tooth*—back to Dr. Hashigami's family? If I did, I'd feel a lot better.

But I quickly rejected the idea. If I gave up the key, I was doomed. That was how it felt. If only I could sneak into his house.

The idea suddenly came to me. If it was his key, the most likely place to find the keyhole was in his lab, or in his home. But there was no way I could visit his home right now. Actually, I didn't even know where it was.

"Why... Why is this happening to me?" No matter how many times I tried to force it in, it wouldn't fit.

I pressed down on it too hard and my hand slipped. I dropped the key. I quickly fell to the ground and began to search for it. By the time I finally found it and picked it up, I realized that several pedestrians were looking at me suspiciously.

Eyes. Eyes. Eyes.

Their eyes pierced me.

"S-stop it..." A cold sweat ran down my back. "Don't look at me..." I hurriedly stood up and ran away. I needed to shut out any information from the outside.

Ignore their gazes. Nobody was staring at me. I'm fine. I'm fine. I'm fine.

I kept walking and mumbling to myself. I headed home as fast as I could, being careful to take as many empty streets as possible.

It was dark. It was like I was walking through an endless darkness. I wanted to be alone, but I was afraid of being alone. How long had I been walking? Maybe I wasn't in the real world anymore.

I suddenly heard a violent flapping of wings from the sky. It was too loud to be crows. I looked up in shock and saw something coming down.

A person? No, this was a devil. I knew that instinctively. He was dressed all in black, and in the darkness, it was hard to make him out. The one thing I could see clearly were two eyes, the crimson color of blood. There was a wicked light within them that was staring straight at me. I could also see two big, symbolic wings on his back.

"A devil..."

The wings were featherless and shiny, and reflected a little of the starlight. I didn't know why, but I was staring at exactly what I imagined a devil to be.

Terrified, I tried to turn and run away. I screamed...or tried to scream, rather. My voice didn't come out. A fierce electric numbness ran through my body. It was a hundred—no, a thousand—times worse than static electricity. It was like when I was shot with Ryotasu's

Poyaya Gun. The shock raced through my whole body.

I was cold.

A moment ago I'd been surrounded by cold air, but this was a whole different kind of chill. It was like being doused in freezing water. It didn't feel cold. It felt painful. My body was literally freezing solid. I could feel the sensation fading away from my hands and feet.

I couldn't move. I couldn't move my hands, my feet, my mouth, or even my eyeballs. I could just make out the devil saying something in front of me, but all I heard was the sound of grinding teeth.

The devil brought its face right up in front of me. Its breath was so hot I thought it would burn my cheek. It put a sharp-clawed hand on my chest. It was going to take my heart—

I wanted to scream, but I couldn't. As I watched in helpless despair, the devil laughed a little and ran through my body.

Frozen like a statue, I lost my balance. My body shook, tilted, and fell. I could see the ground getting closer. And when I struck the asphalt, my body shattered into a million pieces—

I leapt up. In fact, I leapt up so hard that I fell out of bed.

I was in my room. I was panting violently because it was hard to breathe. My throat was parched. But I didn't have the energy to go get any water, so I just lay on the floor for a while in shock.

I looked at the clock, and it was past 9:00 AM. It was light outside. I was late for school. Not that it mattered, since I hadn't been going lately.

I could hear the sounds of helicopters in the distance. They were really loud.

"So it was all a dream, huh?"

Ever since the night of Dr. Hashigami's murder, I'd been having

nightmares. Sometimes I thought things would be so much nicer if it were all just a dream.

I was soaked with sweat. My shirt was damp and clinging to my skin. And wait, it felt really warm near my crotch. I didn't...

I tried my best to deny it, but when I ran my hand down to my pants...

"Aaah! You peed your pants. That's so embarrassing! Eeyahaha!"

"Huh?"

I could hear a girl's voice coming from the Skysensor next to my bed. I couldn't believe what I was hearing. This was the voice of the girl who'd told me to pull out the professor's tooth!

I quickly clung to the radio. The Zonko strap I'd tied to it slowly shook.

"T-this isn't a dream, right?!"

"That you peed your pants?"

"Y-you! You! You're talking to me, right?"

"Don't worry about me. Just turn on the TV! Something really bad's happening!"

"I'm worried about you! What are you? Because of you, I—"

"Shut up and turn on the TV! Quick!"

There was no room for disagreement. I had no choice but to obey.

I wasn't even allowed to change before I took the bag with the radio to the living room. Mom must've already left because she wasn't here. I picked up the remote and turned on the TV.

"—The police have just made their announcement! They've already found f-fifty-one bodies! *Fifty-one!* And they say they're going to find more!"

"Huh?!"

The female reporter's voice was almost a scream. I recognized exactly where she was. It was Inokashira Park. But the park didn't seem peaceful like it always did. Police officers were running around, and in the distance I could see lots of media people. There were blue tarpaulins everywhere, and you couldn't see the lake in the park. Something crazy was happening. That much I knew.

"I repeat! Early this morning, at least fifty bodies were discovered in the lake in Inokashira Park! There are believed to be over a hundred more down there as well!"

Fifty bodies? A hundred more? A chill ran down my back. "What the hell is going on?"

PARANORMAL SCIENCE NVL
Occultic;Nine
オカルティック・ナイン
THERE IS NO SUCH THING AS THE "OCCULT." IT CAN ALL BE DISPROVED BY SCIENCE.
ONLY THOSE WHO HAVE ACCEPTED EVERYTHING
HAVE THE RIGHT TO KNOW THE TRUTH.

▸ site 34: Kiryu Kusakabe

You know what the world of the dead is like? There are lots of wannabe psychics and high-and-mighty philosophers who'll tell you all sorts of crap about it, but they're all full of shit. Everything you've seen about the spirit world in movies, in manga, in books? It's all so totally wrong, it's laughable. Barely any living humans know what it's like after you die.

But—and this is important—there are a few people out there who do. I'm one of them, actually. Why do I know what it's like, you ask? I don't even have to explain. The reason is 'cause, again and again, I've died.

The first day I died, it was way too goddamn hot, and the cicadas were annoying as hell. When it happened, this fake version of me showed up out of nowhere. For a second, I thought I had split in two, but I quickly realized I was wrong. The other me was still asleep, and he wasn't getting up.

That's when I realized...the other me wasn't my double. I was *dead.*

Well, it wasn't that complicated to figure out. What had happened was obvious enough that even a shithead like me could get it. Honestly, the fact that I'd thought I'd split in two, even for a second, just goes to show that I've got the brains of a monkey.

I'd committed suicide. As a result, my spirit had left my body, I guess. I'd thought I'd died, but all I'd done was separate my body and soul. I was able to quickly get back into my body. Ironically, it was after I died that I started to really think about my life a little.

After that, by the way, I died a bunch more times, and each time I was able to go back to my body. After trying it a bunch of times, I finally realized how fucking crazy this power is. People say that if you're willing to die, you can do anything, and man, have they got that right.

One time, I was outside my body having fun, and I stayed out a bit longer than I'd intended. I was away from it for like two weeks. And even then, I didn't have any problems.

It does put a lot of stress on my body, though, so I can't do it that often. If you do it too much, the next day your joints hurt so much you can't get out of bed. You'd think your bones had all fused together. If I did it for too long, I might die for real. Never tried that, though.

Oh, and there's one more thing. I don't quite get how this works, but time flows differently when you're a ghost and when you're in the real world.

It's strange, but what feels like a long time as a ghost isn't that much time at all in the real world. I've come up with this theory that when I'm a ghost, I'm seeing the future at an incredible speed. And when I get back to my body, barely any time's passed at all. You might not believe it, but I mean, we're talking about ghosts to begin with. Who knows how *any* of this shit works?

So anyway, here's where it gets interesting. A few years ago, I was near Musashi-Seki on the Seibu Shinjuku Line, doing one of my "wandering experiments." It was pretty late, and all the houses around me had their lights off.

Then I ran into this girl. It was cold as shit, but she didn't have a coat on, or any shoes, and she was just kind of staggering down the road. I got curious and followed her, and I see this dumb bitch is about to duck under a guardrail and fling herself in front of a fucking train. The train's coming down the tracks, and the conductor's blaring the warning siren as loud as he possibly can.

I don't have the slightest idea why, but even with all this noise I can hear exactly what she's saying. I can hear her even though she's got her mouth closed. It was probably the voice of her heart, I think.

Anyway, so I can hear her. It's the one time I ever really felt like a ghost.

I didn't know the details, but the girl's about to kill herself. She keeps telling herself that if she dies, she'll be happy.

I may be a ghost, but even I don't much feel like seeing a girl get ground to mincemeat by a goddamn train. So I try calling out to her with my mind. It's the first time since I became a ghost that I've tried this.

And then...

This girl hears me, even though I ain't even really there, and do you know what she calls me? She calls me a devil! Man, I was laughing my ass off! And the bitch of the thing is this: she calls me a devil, but instead of being afraid, she likes me! Talk about a crazy-ass suicidal bitch! But eh, I ended up kind of liking being called a devil.

That's when my relationship with the girl began. It was a pain in

the ass to keep up a conversation with this crazy chick all the time, but one day she comes to me and says she wants to open a "Black Magic Agency." And then I get an idea.

There's money here, I think.

I mean, this girl's got a real devil on her side. Y'know, *me.*

The chick's a bit of a drama queen, actually. A drama queen with a vivid imagination. Sometimes I wonder if she ain't hypnotizing herself somehow. She never doubts me.

Maybe that's why I've been able to stay her partner for almost two years. But lately, things have been getting a little strange around me. My bad feeling started around the time this guy Hashigami's hair showed up in the House of Crimson's mailbox. The girl was starting to freak out, and that was a pain in the ass for me.

At this rate, she might break the deal, and then I'd lose my golden goose. So what to do?

First, I'd start by finding out who these people were who were trying to find out about her. Of course, I'd have her help me.

And so I go to her shop, and for the first time, she starts saying some weird stuff.

"I can hear your voice more clearly than usual this morning, I think."

"No shit, huh? Interesting." I almost burst out laughing. "Yeah, I bet you can. Heh."

But I didn't give a crap.

PARANORMAL SCIENCE NVL
Occultic;Nine
オカルティック・ナイン
THERE IS NO SUCH THING AS THE "OCCULT." IT CAN ALL BE DISPROVED BY SCIENCE.
ONLY THOSE WHO HAVE ACCEPTED EVERYTHING
HAVE THE RIGHT TO KNOW THE TRUTH.

▸ site 35: Toko Sumikaze

I came into work at my usual time, and the whole office was in an uproar. It was even worse than when Dr. Hashigami died. Nobody was working. Some people were glued to the TV, some were sitting on the internet looking things up, and others were calling every expert they knew.

What was going on? Had something big happened? I was running a little late that morning, so I hadn't really seen the news.

I took off my coat and headed to the sofa we used for guests, where the editor-in-chief was sitting. That was where the biggest TV in the editorial office was.

"Good morning. What happened?" But even when I spoke to him, the editor-in-chief just nodded a little and turned back to the TV screen. There were ten or so other editors around him, and they all had serious looks on their faces.

I turned my eyes to the screen. There was some text in the top left. When I read it, I couldn't believe my eyes.

"Over seventy bodies found in Inokashira Lake"

"What? Seventy?"

They'd found seventy bodies? Was Inokashira Lake even that big? It couldn't have been very deep.

And that park was pretty busy, even on weekdays, and right near Kichijoji Station. They'd found seventy bodies in a place that was frequented by that many people? Was that possible?

The TV screen was showing an aerial shot of Inokashira Park. There was a male reporter aboard the helicopter, trying his best to remain calm (and utterly failing). "It's been three, no, four hours since the first body was found. The scene is in chaos as even more officers arrive. You can see the whole of the park from up here, and you can see officers on boats pulling up bodies. Many of them seem to belong to women and children. This can only be described as a nightmare!"

Just like the reporter said, I could see police pulling bodies out of the water. They were all fully clothed. It was so terrible I couldn't speak.

Often, drowned bodies will build up gas in their stomachs and swell, but I couldn't see many bodies like that here. Maybe it hadn't been that long since they'd died.

"Can they really show those bodies?" the editor-in-chief whispered.

At the exact same time, as if he'd somehow heard him, the reporter on screen turned to the camera with teary eyes and yelled. "Cameraman, try not to show the bodies! They keep ending up onscreen! We can't let the viewers see that—"

And then the screen cut away. This time it was showing a female reporter inside the park. "We just got new information in! The police have now discovered over a hundred bodies! That's right, the police say they've found over *one hundred bodies!*"

"Ascension..." A hundred. It didn't seem real.

"There are still more bodies at the bottom of the lake, and in the end, they say it's likely there will be over two hundred. They're having trouble pulling them all out, and no luck at all identifying them so far." And then there was another loud sound, different than the sound of the helicopter rotors above. "Look! Is that... Is that an excavator?! It's inside the park! It's heading for the lake!"

"Wait, don't tell me they're planning to dredge the lake with that thing!" the editor-in-chief yelled. "There are still bodies down there! No, not just bodies! There might be something important down there that tells us what the hell happened! And they're going to dredge it with heavy equipment? Are the police stupid?!"

That was a very *Mumuu* way to look at things, but he was right. This whole thing was crazy. It was best to preserve as much of the scene as possible. But for some reason, the cops were putting all their effort into getting the bodies up as fast as they could.

"What happened?! Why are there so many bodies?!"

Nobody answered me. Everybody else watching the TV was thinking the same thing I was. This was insane.

From the look of the damage to the bodies shown onscreen, they hadn't been dead that long. That would mean that in a very short period of time—a day or two, probably—over a hundred bodies had suddenly appeared in that lake.

"Is this an occult phenomenon, you think?" I asked the head editor, fearfully, but all he did was nod. Nothing else.

It wasn't good to make guesses. Maybe we needed more information first. I brought my laptop from my desk and connected to the internet.

How had they found all these bodies to begin with? When did they die? I wanted to know. I hit up all the news sites.

"Over Fifty Bodies Found in Inokashira Lake"

"Still More Bodies Found in Lake, Possibly Over Two Hundred"

As I followed the related story links, I kept seeing headlines like that. It looked like even the police and media didn't really have details yet. But despite that, foreign news sites like CNN and Reuters had already put up their own articles.

Just for the hell of it, I hit up one of the aggregator sites. There was barely any information out yet, but the 2channel newsboards were filled with threads, and a real internet festival was underway.

I opened one of the aggregator sites just to see what I'd find.

"Over Fifty Dead Bodies Found in Inokashira Lake"

At around 6:00 AM this morning, at Inokashira Park in Mitaka, Tokyo, the police received a report of a body floating in the lake. An investigation revealed the body of a man in his twenties or thirties in Inokashira Lake. In the same area, five more bodies of men and women were found, and the Musashino police sealed off the park and began a more thorough search. By 8:00 AM, over fifty bodies had been found, but it seems that there are still more below.

2: Anonymous Reporting Live

> Da fuq? Fifty?

8: Anonymous Reporting Live

> WHHAAATTT?? THERE'S THAT MANY BODIES IN THE LAKE? SINCE WHEN? SINCE WHEN?

9: Anonymous Reporting Live

> The hell? I was just there yesterday and I saw nothing!

10: Anonymous Reporting Live

> I went out there last year with my girlfriend on a boat. It did smell kinda bad, come to think of it.

12: Anonymous Reporting Live

> And there's probably more. Holy shit. How many do you think they're gonna find?

13: Anonymous Reporting Live

> Japan's fucked. See you guys.

16: Anonymous Reporting Live

> Anytime there's a disaster, they start off by saying, "There are only a few casualties," and then it goes up from there, right? Same thing as that. They haven't confirmed a bunch, so the number's still small, that's all. It's gonna go up. Only when the coroner looks at the bodies and says they're dead does an "unbreathing body pulled out of the water" turn into a corpse. The bodies are all lined up in front of the coroner right now, waiting for their turn.

17: Anonymous Reporting Live

> What's about to happen to us?

21: Anonymous Reporting Live

> This is crazy. This is really crazy. I'm so scared I'm going to piss myself.

24: Anonymous Reporting Live

> Who killed all these guys? This is way more than one guy on his own could kill, dumbass.

25: Anonymous Reporting Live

> >> 24
> Nobody said they were murdered. Take the hint. Hint: You're the dumbass.

26: Anonymous Reporting Live

> So what, you're telling me it's an accident?! Then what kind of accident was it? If anything's impossible, it's that. Be realistic.

31: Anonymous Reporting Live

> It's gotta be God in Inokashira Park. Did you know that God's there?

32: Anonymous Reporting Live

> Think it might be some kind of curse? There's been a lot of nasty stuff going on in Kichijoji for a while now.

35: Anonymous Reporting Live

> >>31
> Nobody wants to talk about that. I'm bored of that shit, anyway.

36: Anonymous Reporting Live

> Nobody here actually thinks that this was just a series of accidents, right? That's absolutely impossible. There has to be somebody behind this.

54: Anonymous Reporting Live

> >>36
> Not necessarily someBODY. It could be someTHING, right? We

should consider the possibility of vengeful spirits, a curse, or some kind of shamanistic element.

61: Anonymous Reporting Live

Did you guys know? Every year, about 80,000 people go missing in Japan. 98% of them are found, but the other 2% never are. You know what I'm getting at, right?

63: Anonymous Reporting Live

IT'S A TENGU! A TENGU DID IT!!!

67: Anonymous Reporting Live

A friend of a friend was saying, actually, that Inokashira Park was dangerous and that you should avoid it. Supposedly, if you've got a sixth sense, you can tell immediately.

71: Anonymous Reporting Live

They just drained the water from the lake and did a big cleaning a while ago, right? When was that?

75: Anonymous Reporting Live

>>71
Yeah, that's right. They did it in 2014. It was on the news. Of course, nobody found any bodies then.

81: Anonymous Reporting Live

There were a ton of bikes down there, remember? If there were that many bikes, you could actually maybe fit 100 people down there. The water's dirty, so you can't see the bottom, after all.

83: Anonymous Reporting Live

Are you stupid? There's no way. Idiots like you are how conspiracy theories spread.

84: Anonymous Reporting Live

Where'd they die, and how'd they get into the lake, you think??!!!
Somebody tell me!! Tell me! HOLMES!

89: Anonymous Reporting Live

No way one guy kills 50 people. Is there some kind of mafia or cult or secret society involved? I've never heard about anybody like that over there.

93: Anonymous Reporting Live

If it was some kind of group, what crazy ritual were they doing, you think? This isn't the middle ages. What could they be summoning that needs that many sacrifices?

...

Could it be...SATAN?!

95: Anonymous Reporting Live

That's scary as fuck... I'm never leaving my room again.

97: Anonymous Reporting Live

>>95
Stay in your room your whole life, NEET.

99: Anonymous Reporting Live

>>97
You can stay home and do solo hide-and-seek, and you might still go missing! Even being a NEET isn't safe!

112: Anonymous Reporting Live

I'm seriously thinking it's ghosts.

120: Anonymous Reporting Live

I could see maybe a killer stalking the street at night, and each day he kills one person and throws their body in the lake. Dunno if that killer's human or inhuman, though.

126: Anonymous Reporting Live

Dead bodies float, don't they? Everybody knows that. But they never found the bodies until this morning. And there's nothing on them to indicate that they were tied down. Which means you've got one of two options.

• For some reason, the bodies weren't floating even though they weren't weighed down.

• There were no bodies in the lake yesterday, and they all appeared in a single night.

Either way, what the hell? There's no way to explain that without supernatural intervention.

130: Anonymous Reporting Live

Did anybody from 2chan ever want to meet up there? I bet you could find something if you checked the backlogs. Like, maybe somebody set up a group suicide from here, or something like that?

133: Anonymous Reporting Live

>>130

Get thee to the Occult Boards! They're filled with that shit. "Let's all meet in real life and summon a dangerous spirit," or, "Let's meet in real life and face off with a demon," or something like that. Or, "Let's go vandalize a haunted area," or stuff. Maybe one of those idiots did something and pissed off the spirits and got themselves killed.

134: Anonymous Reporting Live

> I live in Kichijoji, and I've been hearing ambulance and patrol car sirens all day. Even if there's nothing they can do about that, the media helicopters are annoying as fuck. How many of them are there?

158: Anonymous Reporting Live

> I'm here at Inokashira Park! The cops got pissed and told me not to go in, lol
> The park feels five degrees colder than the rest of the area. Is it my imagination? It's so cold I started shaking. It wasn't this cold five minutes ago.

161: Anonymous Reporting Live

> Actually, I saw the ghost of a soldier at Inokashira Park two months ago!

166: Anonymous Reporting Live

> Is it true that a lot of the media there are just passing out 'cause they're sick?

171: Anonymous Reporting Live

> Why Inokashira Park, anyway? If you wanted to ditch a body, you'd be able to hide it a lot better in the mountains or ocean than in a busy place like that. There must have been some reason they had to put the bodies there. And it probably has something to do with all the weird crap that's been going on in Kichijoji for the last few months.

183: Anonymous Reporting Live

> You mean a ley line or something running under Kichijoji? I've never heard anything like that. Was there any kind of spiritual

connection in that town? I just glanced through the comments and realized that more people than I thought were into occult stuff.

"Maybe every commenter here is a dedicated reader of mine!" I said softly. *No, that doesn't matter.*

There was a vigorous debate going on, but all of them were just guessing. None of them had any useful information. I went back in front of the TV.

The editor-in-chief was using the remote to flip through the channels. Every one of them had interrupted their programming to report on the news.

"I'm here in front of Musashino Police Station." The screen was showing the street in front of the station.

A female reporter was holding a clipboard and looking at the camera with a serious expression.

"There was just an announcement from the police. None of the bodies so far have shown any signs of external trauma. I repeat. None of the bodies found so far have shown any signs of external trauma."

No wounds? Then they were killed by poison or drowning... Or maybe...a curse?

No way. I'd never heard of anyone killing a hundred people with a curse.

"Inokashira Park remains sealed off, and the officers are still doing their best—"

"I saw it! I saw it!" Suddenly, I heard a girl's high-pitched yell from the TV.

The reporter looked surprised, and then turned to look outside the frame. The camera followed her. There was a chubby woman in her early forties coming towards the reporters and shouting something in a loud voice.

This was totally unplanned. The reporters all looked annoyed to have their broadcasts interrupted.

But the woman ignored them and kept on screaming. "Last night! I saw them! There were people going into the lake!"

Was she a witness? The reporters all started to whisper, and all the cameras turned towards her.

"What do you mean, 'going into the lake'? Be more specific!" They started to shout questions at her.

She grabbed one of the microphones that were pointing at her and began to yell, flinging saliva everywhere. "There's nothing 'specific' about it! I live in a condo there, and I saw the whole thing from my veranda on the eighth floor! The park was dark, but I could tell there were people there! It felt like there were a lot of people walking through the darkness. I've been living here for thirty years, and nothing like that has ever happened before! The place is usually empty at night, you see. Sometimes groups of rowdy teens will have parties and stuff, but what happened yesterday was totally different. The whole park was quiet. It was as quiet as it always is, but I could just tell that there were all these people! There's lights at the front of the park, you know?! And I could see all these people walking under them into the park! Just like they were going for a walk! They jumped over the fence and walked right into the lake! While wearing their clothes, too! They went into the lake...and they *didn't come out!*"

What she said didn't make any sense. The woman was very excited, and it was hard to make out exactly what she was saying.

"Do you mean they all killed themselves?" The head editor

whispered as he looked at the screen.

The reporters started peppering her with questions. "Tell us more about the people who were going into the lake."

"There were men and women! And some of them were even children!"

"Do you mean they went into the lake in groups? Groups of how many?"

"No, they went in alone! One at a time!" The woman seemed irritated as she answered. "They all came to the park one by one! And not all at the same time, too! I saw the whole thing from my veranda! It was creepy and scary, but I was so freaked out by it I couldn't sleep! I ended up watching it from 1:00 AM last night until morning! Every five minutes or so, one or two people would walk right in and then go into the lake!"

"What?" Was that...possible?

"Did you count how many there were?!"

"Why didn't you call the police?"

"Call the pol—I couldn't do that! It was... It didn't seem real! I thought maybe they were filming a movie or something! I mean... I mean they all just walked straight into the lake, like it was most normal thing in the world! One at a time, like they were all waiting their turn! Nobody making a fuss! You couldn't even imagine while you were watching it that over a hundred people died!" The woman finally broke down and started to cry.

What she said seemed so unreal that the reporters didn't seem to know what to do. "A-ahem... It appears that this woman is a resident of a condominium near the park," one of them said. "This is all so sudden that we're not sure what to do. The police statement says they're still looking for witnesses. Is this new information then? Um... Let's just send you back to the studio."

But even back at the studio, the newscasters and guest commentators were too shocked to speak. It was impossible to believe what the woman had said, but if it was true, this was a group suicide.

"Um, sir, can we assume this is possibly some kind of group hypnosis?"

"Y-yeah. Anyway, this is huge! Hey, Hirata! Get some people together and get your butts to Kichijoji!" Hirata hurriedly got ready to leave.

"*Mumuu*'s going to cover this?" I asked.

"Huh? What did you say?" the editor-in-chief asked, his eyes still glued to the screen.

"Is *Mumuu* going to cover this? *You're* the one who said we weren't a gossip magazine."

"You can complain after you're done. For now, we need to act, or we won't learn anything!"

"You're right. Should I go, too?"

"Sheesh! What the hell's going on?" He didn't answer. He was lost in thought.

It was true that what the woman had said was clearly something that *Mumuu* should investigate. I'd actually had goosebumps for the last few minutes. "Should I go talk to the woman on the news just now?!" I asked.

"Sumikaze! Get to looking!"

"Oh, right! Understood!"

I'd never seen him in such a hurry before. I quickly got ready to go. There were a bunch of things I wanted to check with the head editor before I left, but he was too busy dealing with others to answer my questions. I gave up and left the editorial office.

PARANORMAL SCIENCE NVL
Occultic;Nine
オカルティック・ナイン
THERE IS NO SUCH THING AS THE "OCCULT." IT CAN ALL BE DISPROVED BY SCIENCE.
ONLY THOSE WHO HAVE ACCEPTED EVERYTHING
HAVE THE RIGHT TO KNOW THE TRUTH.

▸ site 36: MMG

"Explain the meaning of this! Do you think you can get away with something so forceful?" Hatoyama stood up so angrily that his chair almost went flying. It was rare for the normally peaceful Hatoyama to get so worked up.

But in a sense, it was to be expected. The Inokashira Lake incident was even more of a surprise to them than the Dr. Hashigami matter. Takasu, standing across from the men, was the only person in the room who was calm. Because—

"Takasu, is it true that you did this all of your own volition?!" Matoba said, with a stern look on his face.

Takasu nodded without changing his expression. "That's true."

"Who the hell do you think you are?! You may be the man in charge of this project, but that doesn't mean you can get away with doing whatever you want!"

"You're the one who said that we could get away with being a little forceful, Mr. Hatoyama. We had a choice to continue or discard the experiments. And I thought that we'd come to a mutual understanding as to which was our priority. In light of our objective, I decided that this was the appropriate response." Takasu didn't get angry, nor did he beg for mercy. It was as if he was saying that there was nothing wrong with what he'd done.

"The plan was supposed to be to move to Phase Two in stages. You can't just ignore that and discard the entirety of Phase One! That's insane!" Most of the seated men seemed just as upset as Hatoyama.

Takasu realized this, and sighed. "If you just let your guinea pigs run free, sometimes they might bite," he began in his usual dramatic voice. No one seemed to know quite what to make of this. "You're free to call them 'high-spec,' if you like, but I see things differently. Our feral guinea pigs are a threat to the entire plan itself. The bugs in the first generation had only been found in a few individuals so far, but that was just an early warning sign. Given time, there was plenty of chance that the number might rise to two digits, or three. Think of a cage filled with guinea pigs, and then a few of them get sick. If you leave them alone, soon the rest will be sick as well. There was a need to deal with things rapidly."

"And so you destroyed the whole cage, is that it?" Hatoyama's words were a cross between a question and a moan.

The decision was such an extreme one that there was no easy way for the seated men to tell if it was right or wrong.

"It makes sense, but..." Matoba, a doctor and a scientist, attempted to express his reluctant understanding, but Hatoyama was still unsatisfied.

"Even making allowances for that, so many people, all at once? Even *I* can't cover you there. You've gone too far on your own."

"Do we need a moment of silent prayer, perhaps?"

Hatoyama gritted his teeth at Takasu's provocations. "I'm not here to discuss the value of the guinea pigs' lives. You know damn well how many people are involved in the cleanup each time something happens."

"There's no need for you to trouble yourself with anything. The mind control via the 'occult' is still working just fine. Weren't you the one who said that?"

"..."

"The Japanese put a higher emphasis on 'fitting in' than on any other factor, no matter how insane the situation around them may be. Am I wrong?"

No one complained.

Takasu looked at their expressions as if enjoying it, and then said in a loud voice, "The first generation has finished their role. We will move up our original plans and advance to the second phase."

Paranormal Science NVL
Occultic;Nine
オカルティック・ナイン
There is no such thing as the "Occult." It can all be disproved by science.
Only those who have accepted everything
have the right to know the truth.

▶ site 37: Yuta Gamon

"Death Toll at Inokashira Park Rises to 256 Victims, Investigation Ended"

From Asayomi Newspaper

Yesterday, multiple bodies were discovered inside Inokashira Park. The Musashino police have spent the last day doing a full search of the park, and have come to the conclusion that the total number of victims is 256.

Attempts to identify the bodies are currently underway. Right now, thirty-four have been identified.

The majority of the victims drowned to death, and none suffered any external trauma. The Musashino Police Department stated that as no crime had been committed, they do not plan to investigate the matter further.

■NEET God

> Huh? No crime? Is that some kind of joke?
> Sure didn't see that coming lolol
> The media seems intent on using the mass hypnosis theory to control public opinion

What do you losers think? Okay, Basariters, go ahead and rip this thing apart.

1: The Anonymous Samurai

This is some crazy shit. Frost Prist.

3: The Anonymous Samurai

I lol'd at the no crime thing. It's so obviously a cover-up.

10: The Anonymous Samurai

The number 256 is no coincidence. Somebody definitely picked that number. This isn't an accident.

14: The Anonymous Samurai

So they aren't investigating it? They're really not gonna look at it at all? The cops can't expect to get away with this shit.

20: The Anonymous Samurai

It's actually weirder how fast they made that decision. They could at least look for a little. They dredged the lake but there's no sign of them looking at anything else. So how can they be sure it wasn't a crime?

22: The Anonymous Samurai

No crime = accident
Good, so much for the Kichijoji mass murderer, right? Good news. Good news.

31: The Anonymous Samurai

If this is an accident, what happened? Poison gas? Mass food poisoning? Doesn't it make no sense that they aren't explaining that?

35: The Anonymous Samurai

> It's a conspiracy! I smell a conspiracy!

42: The Anonymous Samurai

> >>31
> Poison gas is a no-go. They said the cause of death was drowning. Not that I believe them, lol

43: The Anonymous Samurai

> Even if the cause of death was drowning, that doesn't mean there wasn't gas. Maybe they ran into the water to escape the gas? Even if it was poison gas, it's too early to assume it was a terrorist attack. There's a possibility the gas came out from underground. It's weird that the paper said "mostly drowned," too.

48: The Anonymous Samurai

> If they were able to give Inokashira a thorough search, there should be a police announcement. One saying there was no poison gas found, right? If there was gas it would be clinging to the plant leaves and stuff. There's a zoo and an aquarium in Inokashira Park too, so of course, the animals would die as well. But there's been no announcement. So there's no poison gas.

52: The Anonymous Samurai

> Well, the mainstream media's mass hypnosis theory makes sense, right?

55: The Anonymous Samurai

> The problem is where did that hypnosis come from? Or did these 256 people get together somewhere and get high on something?

57: The Anonymous Samurai

You guys love your conspiracy theories. It's easy to assume that mass hypnosis implies something evil, but there is such a thing as the placebo effect. We should also consider the possibility of innocent mass hypnosis affecting the subconscious. It doesn't have to have been a cult or a fortune-teller either, there's a chance they could've been hypnotized at a concert. At clubs they play lots of music at just the right tempo to put the audience in a trance. It's the same thing as that.

58: The Anonymous Samurai

It's not impossible, but it sure as hell ain't likely. And I've heard that brainwashing and hypnosis can't kill people. It can't lead people to do things they don't want to do.

61: Sounds Like Bad News ◆iQ1CwzKqLM

>>58
There's examples of cults committing mass suicide, like at that one temple. Doesn't it depend on the environment and mental state of the person being hypnotized?

52: The Anonymous Samurai

The way hypnosis works, the person won't obey any orders they don't want to follow. You'd need a big facility and a lot of time to do group hypnosis on over 200 people. You'd lock them all away from the outside world and have them live as a group, and gradually put them under more and more psychological stress. That's the only way you could get an order to "kill yourself" to work. That's basically what we call brainwashing.

64: The Anonymous Samurai

>>61
You mean "The People's Temple"? BTW I seriously suggest not googling it. I mean it. Definitely don't watch the video. I'm not shitting you.

65: Sounds Like Bad News ◆iQ1CwzKqLM

>> 64
I was avoiding the real name deliberately.
.
.
Don't blame me for what happens.

67: The Anonymous Samurai

If there was some kind of meeting or concert held around that time in Kichijoji, shouldn't they be looking at that? Do you think the cops did?

69: The Anonymous Samurai

There's the little theaters in Kichijoji. If you filled up Mitaka or Ogikubo, that would be a pretty big number.
>Meetings and Concerts

72: The Anonymous Samurai

There's that Black Magic Agency run by that crazy chick in Harmonica Alley, you guys know that? Maybe she went through each person and put a curse on them?

73: The Anonymous Samurai

Black Magic lolol
KiriBasa's gone to the dogs huh? If you're just some occult fan, spend six months lurking.

74: The Anonymous Samurai

>>72

I know the Black Magic Agency! It's really shady, but I actually saw someone going in sometime!

76: Sounds Like Bad News ◆iQ1CwzKqLM

The name's not Black Magic Agency, it's the House of Crimson.

http://www. rouge_small_castle.co.jp/

77: The Anonymous Samurai

What is this? It's scary! This is some bad news.

78: The Anonymous Samurai

>>76

The owner's name, lol

ARIA KURENAINO

That's the most ridiculous name I've ever heard.

79: The Anonymous Samurai

Wait, isn't it actually a little weird that nobody's talking about a mass murderer? Aren't we all just letting the cops and media control us?

80: The Anonymous Samurai

Is it possible for one guy to kill 256 people? For instance, maybe it's possible if he wandered the streets at night and sunk one person in the lake a night?

82: The Anonymous Samurai

Japan's cops aren't that bad. You couldn't get away with that for 256 nights in a row.

84: The Anonymous Samurai

> Aria might be able to pull it off, maybe.

85: The Anonymous Samurai

> If he kept dumping bodies in the lake for days the gas in their bodies would expand. There's carp in that pond, right? Wouldn't they be eaten?

88: The Anonymous Samurai

> Think maybe it's some organization behind it?

92: The Anonymous Samurai

> Seems unlikely. I don't know why they'd want to dump 256 bodies someplace so obvious.
> It's a warning of some kind? Once they've identified all the bodies, think they'll find something they have in common?

93: The Anonymous Samurai

> They probably drove a dump truck up in the middle of the night and dumped them in the lake. I'm sure someone will testify that they saw it eventually. It's too early for the cops to call off the search otherwise.

94: Brought to you by Anonymous

> That batty old hag's testimony was such BS that the cops and media aren't sure how to handle it, I bet.

95: Brought to you by Anonymous

> You think it's worth looking into the suicide by mass hypnosis thing then?

96: NEET God

> lol lol look at you guys lol
> You're supposed to be Basariters and you're believing in all this occult shit lolololololol
> did you convert to a new religion? lolololol

I pounded my fingers hard into the laptop keyboard. I smashed the "l" and "o" keys on my computer expressionlessly, then did a little cheer.

"Man, this mass suicide in Inokashira is the perfect way to make Kirikiri Basara those sweet, sweet affiliate bucks! This is sure to get some big numbers! I'm so glad I live in Kichijoji, haha. Things are looking up for the NEET God, also known as me! I bet I'll have enough money to take Ryotasu to Wood...Busters? Lovers? Bearers?" I took a gulp of the drink (water, naturally) that Master Izumin had poured me.

Usually, I just wrote the article and watched the Basariters debate in the comments, but this time I'd gotten so excited, I'd written a comment of my own. What I'd said was true. Kirikiri Basara was an occult aggregator blog, but the Basariters were expected to deny any belief in the occult and write nasty comments about the articles. Of course, they were expected to deny it all without proof.

And yet...

"They're letting the media control public opinion? I mean, sure, the media's been pushing this whole occult thing lately. 2chan, Yahoo Comments, and Twitter are all full of morons talking about how scary the occult is. If you ask me, it's just a sign of how stupid the Japanese have gotten. If they don't get their act together, even an incident with 256 suicides—we'll call it the 256 Incident—isn't going to bring me any hits," I muttered into my laptop.

I could feel someone looking at me. I looked around the inside of Blue Moon and saw two girls and a...*something*...near the counter, watching me from a distance.

"Come on! Ryotasu, Myu-Pom, Master Izumin, why are you looking like that? You look like you've seen a ghost."

"You're just freaking me out a little," Master said with a wink, the creepy freak.

"Master I understand, but Ryotasu, Myu-Pom, you two are Basara Girls. Come over here and help."

"You sure are enthusiastic about this, Gamo..." Myu-Pom seemed a little nervous.

"You haven't come around for a while, and then you just show up with the same amount of energy. It's a little surprising," Izumin said.

"That's right. You've never skipped out on this place for a whole week, have you?"

"W-were you worried about me, Myu-Pom?"

She smiled, if a little indifferently. "Hmm... I guess?"

"*I* was worried about you!"

It's time to ignore creepy Master Izumin.

"Wow, Myu-Pom was worried about me! I'm so glad I decided to become the NEET God! You didn't seem like you were looking so good, and I guess that's why!"

"But Gamo..." Myu-Pom suddenly looked serious. "I don't think it's good to make fun of what happened."

"Huh? But this is what Kirikiri Basara has always done. Of course, I know that makes me a bad person, but all the aggregator sites are basically doing the same thing."

Even non-occult sites were covering this thing. And beyond that, even the media was only talking about it because they wanted to pull in more viewers and ad dollars.

"A-and don't you think it's weird?" I continued. "I mean, why does everybody on TV and the net think it's some kind of occult thing? It just doesn't make sense."

"It does make sense, though, doesn't it? The occult's been really popular lately," Master Izumin said, as he wiped down the glasses.

"And you'd be happier if there was a big occult fad, right, Gamota?"

"That's right, but there's somebody pushing the occult angle from outside the media. I mean, it's obvious it's the government, right? It's the same as the fashion industry! You know, every season, the fashion magazines and apparel makers get together and decide in advance what the trends are going to be. Then they put it all in magazines for dumb girls to buy. And then the girls end up being convinced that rubber boots and stuff are cute, and then they wear them. Or like, they all wear cardigans off their shoulders. I've thought sometimes that eventually they're going to start wearing military gloves and thinking those are cute, too. Hahaha!"

Now even Myu-Pom looked a little freaked out.

"Gamotan is much, much, *much* more energetic today, isn't he? Five times? Twice? Ten times? A million times!" Ryotasu did an enthralling dance as she spun around. It felt like a while since I'd seen that.

But if I played along, Ryotasu would take that as a cue to start her little act. I decided to ignore the strange dance playing out before me, and share my theories with the three wrong-siders in front of me.

"What I'm saying here is that you can't just believe what the net and the media are telling you. Master, another drink!"

"I've got no intention of believing in ghosts and curses and stuff, but..." Master Izumin poured me another glass of water and put it on the counter. Evidently, he wasn't going to bring it to me.

"We don't even know how these 256 people actually died, right?"

"What are you talking about, Gamota? Didn't you watch the TV? There was some woman who said she saw the whole thing."

"Yeah, I saw her. But is what she said really true?"

"You're saying she was lying?!"

"Was she?"

Both Master Izumin and Myu-Pom's eyes went wide.

"No, I don't know..."

"You don't, huh?" Izumin said.

"But don't you think it's weird that everybody believes what she said? She might just be some woman who wants to be famous. I mean, in more normal circumstances, you'd never believe a woman like that."

Myu-Pom tilted her head. "So you don't believe the theory that it's mass hypnosis by a cult?"

"Well, mass hypnosis is a nice, balanced hypothesis, halfway between occult and reality, I think."

"You sound so arrogant when you say that."

"I'm the NEET God, after all!" I puffed out my chest in pride. "But I don't think the cult thing is right. If there was some kind of cult like that in Kichijoji, they'd probably have caused some kind of trouble with the locals before that."

"I've never seen any news about a cult, yeah," Myu-Pom said.

"Right," Izumin added.

"Then what's your theory, Gamo?"

Ooh, she took the bait. Once I told her my theory, like a detective does at the end of a mystery novel, she was sure to fall in love with me!

"I don't think there was any kind of mass hypnosis. This is…a mass suicide."

"Mass suicide? How's that different?"

"It means that nobody was hypnotized. The thing with conspiracy theories is that they always involve a struggle against an invisible enemy. It's really not that different from being afraid of a ghost's curse. A lot of people just don't realize that."

"Do you realize it? I'm sure you're going to tell me you do, right?" Master sighed as he asked.

I nodded. "I mean, does it make any sense? What would be the point of hypnotizing 256 people into killing themselves? Is there one? Can you think of one?"

"Gamo, calm down."

I'd gotten a little worked up.

"Um, anyway, do you know how many people in Japan kill themselves every year?"

Nobody answered me. Talk about ignorance.

"Thirty thousand. Thirty thousand people."

"That many?" Izumin said.

"So wouldn't it be pretty easy to find 256 people in Tokyo who wanted to kill themselves?"

"Of course not!" Myu said.

"No, I think it would be. This is what you'd say: 'Anybody who wants to commit suicide, let's meet up IRL. After we all have a little party or something, we can take some drugs and kill ourselves at the same spot. If we do that, we can end our lives in a way that'll shock all of Japan!'"

"Gamota, you're completely inappropriate!"

Master's insults didn't exactly make me happy. Insults from Myu-Pom probably would, though.

"So? What happened then?" Myu-Pom was listening to me, her expression serious.

"Well, if they all tried to die at the same time, just given the sheer number of people involved, someone would call the cops before they could do it. So they split up into little groups, and each group died in order. There might even have been people organizing it. Like it was some big event or something."

"Could anyone stay calm enough to do that right before they were going to kill themselves?" Myu-Pom asked.

I nodded. "Anybody who'd go to a meeting like that is someone who isn't brave enough to die alone. If you really want to die, all you have to do is go to the station and jump in front of a train. They didn't do that. But that doesn't mean they didn't want to die at all. By being around a bunch of other would-be suicides, it creates a kind of 'atmosphere.' An atmosphere that says, 'With these guys here, I can die now.' Reading the atmosphere of a room is something Japanese as a race have to do to survive. So this time, they read the atmosphere of the room and died. Hahaha! Talk about irony."

Nobody laughed.

"Since this is basically one big event, there's the participants, and then a volunteer staff. The staff's job is to make sure the event goes off without a hitch." Ryotasu finally decided to join the conversation. She must've been listening while she danced.

"I don't think they were just managing it. I think they wanted to kill themselves, too. Of course, there were probably some people who showed up to kill themselves and didn't go through with it. But don't you think this idea of a casual suicide club makes a lot more sense? I'm planning on publishing this theory on Kirikiri Basara tomorrow."

"I hope Chi didn't..." Myu-Pom looked uneasy.

Ryotasu finished her dance and came up to me. She was panting and maybe sweating a little from dancing. Her cheeks were slightly flushed. "Hey, hey, Gamonosuke. Samurai Gamonosuke Hikojurogorozaemon!"

"Your face is too close. And what's with that weird name?"

"How do you know there's no invisible enemy?"

"Huh?"

Invisible enemy?

When I heard Ryotasu's words, the events at Dr. Hashigami's lab came flashing back to me. I'd almost run into someone there at the lab. While I was trying to yank out the Professor's tooth, I'd heard footsteps out in the hallway. Someone out there had killed Dr. Hashigami, and they hadn't been arrested yet.

What if they'd seen someone yanking out the professor's tooth and running away? In other words, what if they'd seen me? What if they had a lot of friends? What if they were thinking about killing me in order to hide the truth? And what if they couldn't find out exactly who I was, so they decided to start killing all the students at Seimei? What if all the victims from the 256 Incident were from Seimei?

A cold chill ran down my spine. There was no guarantee that I wasn't fighting an invisible enemy.

So...

Could I really be sure the occult wasn't real? I'd always thought that the occult was just a bunch of lies, but now I realized that maybe I was wrong. If radios could talk on their own, then maybe there really could be an invisible enemy.

"Gamotan?"

I started.

Suddenly, I realized Ryotasu's eyes were right in front of my face. She was so close now that I could see my own face reflected in them. Also, her tits were touching my shoulder.

What kind of face was I making right now? Was I still keeping up the face of a scummy affiliate blog admin who only cared about himself? The face I'd worn only a moment ago?

I couldn't let her find out. I needed to keep my face looking normal, and especially around Ryotasu. She knew what had gone on that day. If I didn't want her to suspect me, I had to act normal.

"Th-that's right! There was someone I wanted to introduce you to. Uh... Maybe not some*one*. Some*thing*? Anyway, just look at this. It'll upend your whole world."

I quickly moved away from Ryotasu and turned on the Skysensor, then placed it on a nearby sofa. Ryotasu, Myu-Pom, and Master Izumin looked shocked as I pointed at the Skysensor.

"Get this! This radio talks! And in a girl's voice! Hey, Master Izumin, stop looking at me like I've finally gone crazy." I knelt down next to the radio on the sofa and showed them the Zonko strap hanging from the radio. "Do you know who this is? It's Zonko from MMM. Since I'd thought at first that the strap was talking, I decided to call the voice 'Zonko.' Anyway, listen to this. You'll be amazed."

I turned back towards the Skysensor and poked at the speaker. "Hey, Zonko, you there? I know you're there. Can you say hi to everybody?"

Silence.

The Skysensor was completely silent, so I turned up the volume. *Bzzzzz...zzzzzzz...zzzz...*

I couldn't hear the voice at all. "Huh? Hey, Zonko! Are you asleep? Wait, do you even sleep at all? Do you get up if I turn the power on? Anyway, that doesn't matter. Just answer me. Everybody's waiting." But no matter how many times I spoke into the Skysensor, there was no response at all.

I'd spent the last day or so doing nothing but talking to Zonko. I'd really done nothing but talk to her, honestly. When I tried to go to sleep, she yelled at me and made me talk to her about nothing for a long time after. My idea about the group suicide meeting had come to me only after going over everything with her.

Honestly, I never would've been able to clear my head if I was by myself. Yet now, she wasn't answering me.

"After all that bossing around you did yesterday, how come you're not talking now? Hello!"

"Gamota, here..." Master Izumin put some hot milk on the table. He looked concerned. "Drink this. It's on the house."

He was feeling sympathy! He was looking at me with very sympathetic eyes. And it wasn't just Master Izumin. So was Myu-Pom!

"Zonko-tan? Wakey-wakey! It's Ryotasu! Are you poyaya?" Maybe Ryotasu, at least, believed me, or maybe she was just having fun by imitating me.

"I... I guess Zonko's at school today. Aha...ahahahah..." My excuse echoed futilely off the walls of Blue Moon. *Well, this sucks. Kill me now. I just look like a lunatic!*

My eyes met with the smiling Zonko strap, and I felt like telling her off. "Sheesh... After all that time I spent talking with her, too."

I thought about going to Inokashira Park myself, but there were probably cops there, so I decided not to.

PARANORMAL SCIENCE NVL
Occultic;Nine
オカルティック・ナイン
THERE IS NO SUCH THING AS THE "OCCULT." IT CAN ALL BE DISPROVED BY SCIENCE.
ONLY THOSE WHO HAVE ACCEPTED EVERYTHING
HAVE THE RIGHT TO KNOW THE TRUTH.

▸ site 38: Yuta Gamon

When I got home, I suddenly felt really tired. I must've been more exhausted than I thought.

Of course I was. It was my first time in a week going back to Blue Moon, and I'd been on edge the whole time. I'd been doing nothing but talking to try and hide my nervousness. I knew I was acting differently than usual. Sweat had been pouring out of my whole body.

Ryotasu and Master Izumin were both idiots, so they didn't matter, but...maybe Myu-Pom suspected something was up.

Had Ryotasu told them that I'd gone to see Dr. Hashigami the day he was killed? She hadn't mentioned it at all today.

Even if she was a little stupid, and...*unique*...that didn't mean she wouldn't at least be thinking about it.

"But I don't want to think about it anymore..." There was no good to come from being paranoid. I'd just not be able to believe anything.

I gave up on thinking, took off my coat, and collapsed into bed. I was so tired. Lately I hadn't been sleeping well, and I was exhausted.

And last night, Zonko had kept me up all night.

I wanted to get some sleep today.

I closed my eyes.

But the second I did, Dr. Hashigami's face, the feeling when I'd ripped out his tooth, and the awful smell of the blood came back to me, and it hurt to breathe.

I pulled my blanket over my head. My body started to shake.

"Calm down. Calm down..." I desperately told myself.

"Hey! You! Hey! No sleeping! Gah, if only I could reach out of the radio! I'd tug hard on your sideburns!"

"..." I heard loud, high-pitched yelling coming from the radio. I wasn't sure if that was why, but the flashback to the incident suddenly disappeared.

I sighed and got out of bed.

"You just sighed, didn't you? You do that. But I don't know why you don't like me. You've got a pretty girl like me talking to you. Normally a teenage boy would like that. Are you gay? Or just an idiot?"

"...I don't know how to tell if you're pretty when I can't even see you."

She was less trustworthy than the girls who took selfies on Twitter. In my mind, when she talked, I was envisioning Zonko. But her personality and voice were different from the Zonko in the anime, so there was a little gap in my understanding.

Was that why I felt a little dizzy when I talked to Zonko, or more precisely, the girl on the radio?

"And you know, what were you thinking back there?"

"Back there?"

"At Blue Moon!"

"Oh, I was going to ask you the same thing. You talk to me all the time, so why didn't you say anything back there?"

"Of course I wasn't going to say anything!"

"Why? Were you asleep? Or embarrassed?'

"Why are you telling other people about me? Jeez! You should know better than that, dummy! Dummy-dummy Yuta!"

"Wait, why was I not supposed to do that?"

"For your own sake, Dummy-dummy Yuta."

"What do you mean?"

"If people really thought you could talk to a pretty girl who lived inside a radio, they'd call the cops on you."

"They'd believe me if you talked!"

"No way. There's no way I'm talking, ever."

W-wait, really...?

So Zonko didn't want anybody but me knowing about her.

Well, sure, a mysterious girl who you could talk to on the radio was definitely occult.

"Then at least tell me, now that nobody's around. Who are you?"

Zonko didn't answer.

"How can I talk to you? This radio's got a speaker, but it doesn't have a microphone. It can do output but not input. How are you hearing what I'm saying? And how can you talk when the power's off?"

Zonko said nothing. The Skysensor was silent.

"Hello?" She was ignoring me.

I tried flipping the switch on and off. I even adjusted the volume. But it didn't do any good.

Crap, I must've pissed her off... There was only one thing I could do now.

"Um, Zonko... I'm sorry for being a jerk."

"As long as you understand."

"You were there the *whole time?!*" I resisted the urge to fling the Skysensor out the window.

If this temperamental and (self-proclaimed) pretty girl never talked to me again, I'd be in big trouble.

To be honest, she'd given me someone to talk to over the past two days. That's what had gotten me back on my feet this far.

And...

Without Zonko, by now I'd either be in jail for the murder of Dr. Hashigami, or maybe dead at the hands of the real killer. The only reason I was still safe was the orders she'd given me back in that lab.

Zonko knew something. She knew why Dr. Hashigami was killed, or maybe even who the real killer was... Probably.

My hands gripped the gold tooth key in my coat pocket. This key might be connected to the real killer.

I'd be doomed without Zonko and this key if I wanted to prove my innocence and find the real murderer. I needed to find the connection somehow.

I went to the kitchen and filled a cup with water. And then, for no real reason, I flipped on the TV in the living room.

It was just past 7:00 PM. Most stations were showing variety programs at this hour, but the channel I had on was playing a special on the 256 Incident at Inokashira Park.

A bunch of old men that were identified as "experts" were exchanging theories with serious looks on their faces. In the end, they weren't much different than the aggregator sites. They were making their money off of irresponsibly scaring people.

I was interested in the 256 Incident, but not in the program. I could do a lot better for myself gathering information off the internet.

I changed it to another channel. There were two other news programs on, and they were both running specials on the 256 Incident. It was like the whole world had forgotten about Dr. Hashigami's murder. That was a good thing for me, but somehow it seemed scary, and I shivered.

I went back to my room and opened up my laptop.

"Hey, Dummy-dummy Yuta. Your mom should be home soon, right? It's your favorite tonight, curry rice. Man, I wish I could have some too!"

I was mostly ignoring Zonko's voice.

I typed "Isayuki Hashigami" into the search engine. My fingers were shaking as I did.

For the first week after the incident, I couldn't bring myself to search for the name online. I was too scared. I was terrified that the top hit might be "Yuta Gamon Identified as Murderer," and I just couldn't do it.

But now...I wanted as much evidence as I could get.

I pushed down hard on the enter key. And then I saw a story dated several days ago.

When I saw the video attached to the story, I gasped. It was a video of the funeral at Anyoji Temple, probably from that day's news stories.

I could see several funeral-goers on the temple grounds. A TV reporter was talking into the camera with a grave expression. Then the video changed to show a middle-aged woman and a young man, bowing to the visitors as they held a photo of the deceased. The subtitle read, “Dr. Isayuki Hashigami’s wife and eldest son.” They were covered in camera flashes.

The son was my age, or a little older—maybe a college student. He was a professor’s son, so he must be really smart, too. But the impression I got from watching him was of an exhausted boy trying to act strong. I’d lost my dad too, so I knew how he felt.

I felt another grinding pain deep in my heart.

I should never have looked at this.

I closed the video and looked at the other search results, but I didn’t see any new information about the suspect. That was natural, perhaps.

What about Kirikiri Basara? I hadn’t actually posted any articles about Dr. Hashigami, but several months ago, when he’d made one of his “the occult is real” comments on TV, I’d put up a small article on it. Maybe somebody had put a new comment there.

I opened the article I’d written, desperate for any kind of hint, and...

398: The Occult is FAKE

| In Memory of Long-Haired Hashigami

400: The Occult is FAKE

| If the occult’s real, come back as a Zombie, lolol

415: The Occult is FAKE

| DDDDOOOCCTTORR HASHIGAAMMI!

417: The Occult is FAKE

| So, was the occult real? Or not?

420: The Occult is FAKE

> He kept dodging the point and changing the subject when he got called on something. It pissed me off.
> Glad he's dead.

422: The Occult is FAKE

> So turns out the occult wasn't real, lol

There had only been a few comments over the past few days, and they were all from assholes. I was disappointed to find out that the Basariters were like this. It was worse than scribblings on a bathroom wall.

Annoyed, I smacked my hands on the keyboard.

"Come on, debate! Analyze! You guys are useless! Totally useless!" But—

Then I saw another comment.

446: Hello there, I'm Zenigata.

> So about Hashigami. There was a BL doujin sold at last year's winter Comiket that had a really similar situation to this, I remember. It was Ririka Nishizono's *At the Bottom of Dark Water.* Does that have anything to do with this?

"A doujin...?" My first reaction was to wonder what the hell he was talking about.

In fact, nobody had reacted to his comments, but it did bother me. Part of it was the fact that this was the only decent comment on the page.

Maybe this Nishizono girl had a power like Myu-Pom's, and she was able to foretell what had happened. I wanted to see this doujin for myself.

After that, I acted fast. I skipped school the next morning, and caught the first train to Shinjuku. I went into Tora no Ana as soon as it opened, and searched desperately for *The Bottom of the Dark Water*. It was embarrassing, looking through the BL corner, but I found what I was after.

I scanned through it as soon as I left the store.

It was a doujinshi composed of five short stories by Ririka Nishizono. I'd never read any BL books before, but just like I expected, it wasn't targeted towards boys.

I started reading it thoroughly from the beginning.

The scenes of men in bed together didn't really bother me. Most of the bad stuff was painted out with white. It just looked like two naked, handsome men holding each other and saying creepy shit.

The first story was about bodies at the bottom of the water becoming zombies and climbing back onto land. I thought the Cthulhu Mythos might be involved, but it wasn't. One of the zombie men was called the Devil. First, he had sex with a girl, but then the detective who was investigating the case stole the zombie man away and it turned into a BL thing. Mr. Zombie was a total manwhore.

The second story was called "Kotoribako." It was a tragic love story about an albino boy who carried a box to put little birds in. The boy was a smug asshole who pissed me off. He was having threesomes with twin priests called "Gods of Fortune."

The first two stories had really complicated backgrounds and weren't that good. I started to think that whoever the commenter was on Basara, they were just messing with me. But when I got to the third story, I was shocked.

The third story was another tale of men in love. The two of them were in love and never wanted to part, so (for some reason) one of the men stabbed the other to death with a knife. Then he had sex with the corpse, and—

Ripped out the corpse's tooth as a memento.

That was how it ended.

"It's the same… No, wait, is it?"

Think logically.

The part about the tooth was the same. Even the media had reported that one of Dr. Hashigami's teeth had been removed. If you just looked at the overall situation, it was the same.

But was it really? I hadn't taken the professor's tooth because I was in love with him. And I'd used pliers, not a knife, to get it out.

Taking a tooth out of a corpse was a common theme in detective stories. I tried to tell myself that, but then I read the story again from the start.

"Oh… This…!" And on the page where the man was killed, I saw it. "No… There's no way…" My hands were shaking.

Maybe the Ririka Nishizono girl who wrote this book really had seen the professor's death over two months ago. Or more likely, she was the one who'd killed him.

There was something about the case that the cops hadn't announced yet. The only ones who knew it were people who'd seen the room where he'd died. Me, the real killer, the cops, and maybe the guy who'd found the body? And it was here in this doujinshi.

It was one of the few pieces of information that would lead to the killer that hadn't been publicly announced.

There were four letters in the English alphabet written on a background object in an unobtrusive panel. It was the same as that dying message.

"CODE."

▸ site 39: Miyuu Aikawa

"Did you go to the cops about your friend?"

"Her family said they filed a missing person report," I said as my gaze wandered outside the window.

I was sitting on the second floor of the Excelsior near the entrance to Sun Road, and I could look down and see the people below me clearly. It was late afternoon, so there were lots of housewives doing evening shopping and students heading home from school.

But inside the café, it was mostly female customers. I didn't see anyone but me who was wearing a uniform. Teenage girls like me tended to prefer fast food places like McDonald's.

It was Toko, not me, who'd chosen this place.

I dunno... I felt a little nervous.

The heater was on inside the café, but I felt cold, and I wrapped my arms around myself.

I told myself it wasn't good to worry too much, and tried to take my mind off it, but I couldn't stop thinking about Chi. My mind kept coming back to her.

"Where did she go…?"

Chi was my classmate and best friend. The only reason I'd started "Myu's Niconico Live Fortune-Telling" was because she'd told me to. She'd always helped me with the broadcasts, too. She'd always been there to cheer me up. It was thanks to her that I had the courage to continue this project.

"You okay?" Toko asked.

She had shown up right on time for our meeting, and she'd been worried when she'd seen the look on my face.

It was just like a grown-up woman to be able to be kind without being too obvious. She was really someone I could respect, so I couldn't think of anybody to talk to about this except her.

"So did you find anything?"

"I've been peeking into all the places she used to go every day on the way home from school… But of course, she's not there… I'm not sure what to do…"

"A missing persons report isn't enough to get the police to do anything, yeah…"

I squeezed my hands into tight fists on top of my lap. It had been a week since Chi had vanished. Every day, I kept trying to stop myself from imagining the worst that could happen.

Yesterday I'd finally seen Gamo, who'd been out of touch for a full week too, and so I'd been a little hopeful that maybe I'd see Chi as well.

"When I think about what happened in Inokashira Park, I just get scared. I feel like maybe Chi was one of the people they found down there… I don't really want to think about it, but…" Maybe I shouldn't have listened to Gamo when he was coming up with all his ideas on the case. I started to freak out and ended up coming to Toko for help.

"It's true that they haven't ID'd half the bodies from the lake," Toko commented.

I hadn't looked to see if Chi's name was among the ones they had found. When I thought about seeing her name on that list, I got so scared.

Since I hadn't heard anything from Chi's mom, I'd been telling myself that she had nothing to do with that case.

"Don't think about it too much. Believe, and keep waiting. I know some people with the police, so I'll ask them."

"Yeah...thanks." She was so nice that I wanted to cry, but I bit my lip and stopped myself.

I took a sip of the maple latte she'd bought for me. Its sweetness and warmth made me feel a little better. "I feel a little better, I think."

"I see. I'm glad to hear it." Toko rested her chin on her hands and sighed. "I've been a little busy lately. Maybe I haven't been paying enough attention to what's been going on around me. Somebody I knew died recently, you see."

"..." I gazed out the window halfheartedly. I could see my own sad-looking reflection in the glass.

It reminded me of the vision of the bottom of the water that I'd seen before. Maybe that vision had something to do with the Inokashira Park incident...? No way.

"Hey, Toko. Do people really just...*die* like that?" I didn't even realize what I'd said. "Do you think there's life after death, Toko?"

An editor at *Mumuu* would definitely say yes to that, so I thought it was a bit of an unfair question. I wanted someone to tell me what I wanted to hear, so I'd decided to ask her as opposed to someone else.

"Yeah. Of course there is."

But even so, hearing Toko agree made me feel better.

"I think without the afterlife, the world seems a lot more cramped." Toko smiled a little as she kept talking. "You can replace afterlife with 'heaven' or 'the spirit world,' if you prefer. But I've always wanted to find real, unassailable proof that something like that existed. Something nonreligious, I mean."

"I hope you find it someday, Toko." If she ever did, maybe I wouldn't be scared to die. Maybe I'd be able to really see my dad again.

"Just leave it to me. But when I do find it, I'm charging an entrance fee for all humanity. There'll be no exception for you, Miyuu." Toko puffed out her chest and laughed.

"Oh, I wanted your help with something, Toko."

"What is it? I'm not offering discounts on that entrance fee."

I opened the photo gallery on my phone and showed her a picture.

"What do you think of this?"

She looked at the phone with the stern expression she never let me see.

"Hmm... It's definitely not a ghost photo, I can say that." She stared at it for a while and then smiled a bit.

"It's the last picture that Chi sent me. You see that weird white light, right?" I'd shown it to Toko because she was an editor at *Mumuu* and supposedly had a strong sixth sense.

"I think this is just light bouncing off a cell phone strap or something."

"I see..." I felt a little better hearing that, so that was good. But now my clue was gone.

Toko put the phone on the table, still smiling, and said something strange. "But...I feel a little better," she said,

"You feel better?" I asked.

"Yeah. That's right. About your friend Chi... If there's one thing I can say..."

"..."

"She's still alive."

"What do you mean?"

"If the photo you just showed me really is a clue about Chi, I don't feel any waves of the dead coming from it. You know, I can tell these things."

"Y-yeah..." Her words made me so happy that I teared up a little.

"So you need to get ahold of yourself, okay?"

"Yeah."

"Oh, by the way, Miyuu." When we left the café, Toko turned to me as if she'd remembered something. "Have you been meeting with that guy from Kirikiri Basara lately?"

"Huh? Oh, yeah." I nodded, and Toko adjusted her glasses. The light from the streetlamp flashed off them for a second—or so I thought.

How did Toko know about that? Had she seen the article about me that Gamo had made?

"What's he like?"

"What's he like...?" I never thought she'd take an interest in Gamo. Was it okay to tell the truth...?

"He's kind of a loser. Not the type I'd want as a boyfriend."

Gamo, I'm sorry.

"Does he seem dangerous?"

"Oh, no, not like that. Not at all. Really. Gamo is... Oh, his name is Yuta Gamon. He's a pervert."

"There's lots of perverts in my editorial office, so I'm used to them." Toko started to walk towards the station. As she walked, she asked me about Gamo's age and what he did for a living, and while I hesitated, I answered her.

Eventually she crossed her arms, as if lost in thought, and then pulled me to the side of the street. She stared right into my eyes with a serious look.

"Listen, Miyuu. Can you introduce me to this Gamon kid sometime soon?"

"Huh?"

"He might have something to do with some private research I'm doing."

"Huh? Really? Did he do something wrong?"

"Oh, no. It's not like that. But it feels like a lot of important information goes up on that Kirikiri Basara site of his. I want to talk to him."

"Oh, okay. I'm sure it's fine." Gamo would probably break down in tears of joy if he heard an editor from *Mumuu* wanted to talk to him. At least, he certainly wouldn't turn her down.

"Sorry, I know I shouldn't be asking you things."

I said goodbye to Toko in front of the station and started to walk home.

The instant I was alone, I heard a spooky song from my bag, one you might hear in a suspense movie. This was the melody I used when I got a call from a number not on my contacts list.

I quickly took my phone out of my bag, and sure enough, it was a number I didn't recognize.

"Chi?!" I answered the phone without even thinking about it.

"..."

"Hello?! Is that you, Chi?!"

"..." They said nothing, but I could hear them breathing.

"Hello?! Chi? It's you, right?" I screamed into the phone.

And then...

"Um... No." The voice that replied wasn't Chi's. It belonged to a man.

I was so disappointed I wanted to hang up. But...

"I want to talk to you about my dad."

"Who are you...?"

"Sarai. We talked on your livestreaming program, remember?"

"...!" My heart skipped a beat.

Yeah, I remembered. I'd talked to him on my Niconico Live Fortune-Telling Program a month or so ago.

Gamo had said he was a Basariter, a regular on Kirikiri Basara. He'd pretended to have a question and called in just to humiliate me, but the vision I'd seen was so painful and shocking that I'd cried.

—There's things you want to say to your dad, right? Now's your only chance! If you don't do it right away, you'll really regret it!

That's what I'd said.

And after that, his dad had died. I hadn't been able to speak when I'd seen it on the news. I'd felt a pain in my heart. If I hadn't told his fortune, maybe his dad would've survived.

"Sarai...Hashigami, right?" I knew his name because I'd seen it in the vision.

"...That's right." He didn't seem surprised that I'd guessed his name.

But how did he know this number? The phone number I'd used for my Nico broadcasts was for a different phone that I didn't usually use.

"Oh, I see. You've gone silent for more than a second because you're wondering how I got your private cell phone number, right? It's simple."

He felt like another person who'd be a pain in the butt, in a completely different way than Gamo.

"My father was on TV several times. One of the producers from a show he did came to the funeral. And that producer introduced me to the director of the program you'd appeared on."

Did he mean *Don't Miss It! POM!*?! The world was a smaller place than it looked.

"So you watched the program I was on?"

"No...I googled it."

I-I see. So he didn't know everything, then.

"So...what do you want me to do?"

"Can we meet somewhere?" Sarai said he wanted to talk about his dad.

I remembered the vision I'd seen during my broadcast. It was so noisy that I could only understand fragments of it, and I'd been under so much stress that I think I mixed a lot of it up with memories of my own dad.

Would I be able to answer his questions? Regardless, I felt like I had to talk to him.

"...All right."

PARANORMAL SCIENCE NVL
Occultic;Nine
オカルティック・ナイン
THERE IS NO SUCH THING AS THE "OCCULT." IT CAN ALL BE DISPROVED BY SCIENCE.
ONLY THOSE WHO HAVE ACCEPTED EVERYTHING
HAVE THE RIGHT TO KNOW THE TRUTH.

▸ site 40: Yuta Gamon

"...And so the NEET God thinks that this isn't mass hypnosis, it was a suicide meeting, instead! What do you think, Basariters?" I danced my fingers lightly across the keys, then made a beautiful landing on the enter key to upload my newest article. "Whew. It's been a long time since I uploaded a masterpiece like this."

I'd decided to try uploading my theory about the deaths in Inokashira Park, AKA the 256 Incident, to Kirikiri Basara. Normally, I never uploaded articles just containing my own thoughts. I'd just give out a link to an existing site, add in some inflammatory comments in my role as "NEET God," and then just let things go where they may. That was enough to get the Basariters to start arguing on their own.

"Poyaya? But then why did you decide to make your own 'amazing idea' into an article this time?"

"You wanna know why, Ryotasu? You want me to tell you?"

"Yup. I wanna know why!" Ryotasu nodded as she pointed the Poyaya Gun at me.

I wished, not for the first time, she wouldn't point that thing at people while she was talking to them. It wasn't a toy. It had incredible electrical power. It was actually way more dangerous than your standard air gun.

What idiot gave something so dangerous to a ditzy airhead like her?

"The reason I put my thoughts into an article...was as a warning about the direction the general conversation is going." I grinned.

"A warning? What does that mean?"

"I think we need one. The way Japan's public opinion works, if one person turns right, there's a tendency for everybody else to turn right, too. Everybody wants to fit in. I'm trying say that we need to think about this occult boom that's going on."

"Gamota, that doesn't make sense." Master Izumin was standing on the other side of the counter listening to me, and he interrupted my conversation like always. "That internet thing you do deals with the occult, right?"

I didn't know how old he was, but anybody from the generations before computers had a tendency to call anything done on a laptop "doing an internet thing."

Well, I *was* doing an internet thing, so I decided not to bring it up.

"I'm the admin of an occult aggregator blog. But that's just to get affiliate money. It doesn't *have* to be the occult, if I can make money off it."

"But doesn't that mean an occult boom is good for you? It means people will be more interested."

"KiriBasa is filled with people who hate the occult. It's nice that everybody's getting excited over it, but the whole point of the site is to feel superior by mocking idiots who believe in the occult. Of course, if the occult is popular, that means the debates will get more heated, and I'll get more hits, so of course I welcome it." I tried to look smug as I said it, but Ryotasu poked me in the side and ruined the effect. It made me feel ticklish, so I giggled.

"Jack! Jack!"

"Wh-what? Ryotasu, don't poke me. What's 'jack'?"

"Jack! Jack! Gamotan's a jerky Jack!"

Oh, right. Maybe I am.

The more the Basariters and occult fans engaged in useless debates, the better off I was.

Anyway, I needed this article to get Kirikiri Basara active again. Not being able to upload any articles during the week I was in hiding had hurt me. The other aggregator sites had caught this big wave, and I was falling behind. At this rate, instead of being able to make a living off an affiliate site, I'd wind up running a third-rate site that nobody visited.

"Anyway, that Inokashira incident is full of mysteries, huh?" Master Izumin's muscle-bound body shivered a little. "When I'm at home, I cling to the TV following the latest updates, but there's really nothing. I think that means the cops don't know, either. It's scary. What if I get sucked into the lake too?"

I looked a little on the internet too, and everybody was still talking about the 256 Incident over the past few days.

"Proposal to Drain Inokashira Lake and Conduct a Full Investigation"

"Why Are They Still Having Trouble Identifying the 256?"

"Time of Death for All Fatalities Was Between 9:00 PM the Night Before and 4:00 AM"

"Prime Minister Expresses His Condolences to the Victims of the 256 Incident"

"Public Safety Finds No Evidence of Cult Involvement"

"No Sign of Poison Gas; Theories of Mass Hypnosis Gain Strength"

"Media Wars Heating Up, Local Residents Complain"

"Inokashira Park Closed Indefinitely Until Investigation Complete"

There were headlines like that everywhere.

The latest hot topic was that no one was sure why it was taking so long to ID the bodies. Most of them had died from drowning, and less than twenty-four hours had passed between their deaths and the time of discovery, so the damage to the bodies was almost zero. But the police still had only been able to ID fewer than half. They were dodging the media's questions about why.

And the conspiracy theorists had leapt on that.

As a result, the online debate only got bigger, and now you were seeing occult theories everywhere. Both the media and the internet were ignoring everything else to talk about this.

...The whole world has forgotten about Dr. Hashigami's death.

If the cops were putting all they had into the 256 Incident, that meant they'd be putting less energy into finding Dr. Hashigami's killer. Maybe nobody would realize that I was at the crime scene. But that also meant there was less of a chance that the real killer would ever be found. It also meant that I wasn't going to have a chance to prove my innocence.

My fear of an invisible enemy was growing stronger by the day.

I thought about contacting this Ririka Nishizono person, or maybe telling the police, but that would mean identifying myself, so

I'd hesitated.

Suddenly the door chime rang, and somebody came into the café. Was it the police?! I almost leapt out of my chair. But it was just Myu-Pom.

Don't scare me like that...

"Hello."

"Oh, Myu. Did you get in touch with your friend?"

"Oh, no." Myu-Pom smiled weakly at Master Izumin and then came over to me. "Hi, Gamo."

"Oh, yeah. Hi. It's rare to see you here on a Saturday."

"Um..." She looked like she wanted to say something.

What could it be? A confession of love? No, that couldn't be it. Then...did she want to quit Kirikiri Basara? *Or maybe...*

"Is this about that Myu-Pom special we were going to run on the site? Sorry, I'm too busy with the 256 Incident. And if we wanted to do a special, we'd have to do a bunch of prep work, right? So, wait a while on that."

"..." Myu-Pom looked at me desperately. But in the end—

"No. I understand." That was all she said, and then she went over to Ryotasu.

What was that *about?* I was interested now. I couldn't figure out what girls were thinking. Maybe I should try to make her feel better by telling her we'd do an interview and put a special together sometime soon.

As I wondered about that, I looked at the other article I'd uploaded. There should be comments by now.

I wonder how many comments were posted. If it was just trolls, I'd probably want to kill myself.

There were about ten comments on the article. All of them were posted immediately after my upload, and they all said things like, "Sure, yeah," and, "Too long. Tell me in three lines," or, "Shut up, moron."

I want to kill myself...

"Maybe I should wait a little longer..." If Sarai showed up, the debate would get a little more heated.

Since I hadn't uploaded anything for a while, my regular commenters had disappeared. That might be one of the reasons that my more recent comments were trending more towards the occult.

I sighed and went to close the PC. But then I remembered the comment from "Hello there, I'm Zenigata." about Ririka Nishizono. That was a new comment on an old article. Which meant that maybe the other old articles had new comments on them, too.

I looked at the comment list. I could see that last month's articles on One-Man Hide-and-Seek and the Curse of Kokkuri-san had a decent amount of new comments over the past few days.

"The Curse of Kokkuri-san Is Seriously Terrifying!"

259: Anonymous Is Seriously Scary

> Hey, you know how they've announced the names of the people they ID'd from the Inokashira Park incident? One of them's got the same name as the chick from this article.

260: Anonymous Is Seriously Scary

> >>259
> Lolwut?

261: Anonymous Is Seriously Scary

>>259
How come you know the girl's name? Was it leaked somewhere?

262: Anonymous Is Seriously Scary

>>261
Check the backlog. Basara found her. The name of the school and "around fall" were enough to ID her. They checked the news from that period, and found something that matched.

263: Anonymous Is Seriously Scary

>>At around 7:00 PM on October 13th, a second-year student at Kichijoji Girls' High, Yuna Miyamae (16), collapsed while at school and was taken via ambulance to the hospital. According to reports, she and her friends were doing the "Kokkuri-san" ritual in her classroom. Doctors at Musashino Medical General Hospital say that the cause may have been stress-induced anemia. But is that really all it was?

I found this article in Tokyo Sports, lol
It's really got her name. And it sure sounds like a match, right?

264: Anonymous Is Seriously Scary

Huh? So Yuna died? She wasn't in the hospital?

265: Anonymous Is Seriously Scary

No! Not Yuna! She's our idol!

266: Anonymous Is Seriously Scary

Are you serious... Are you SERIOUS??

267: Anonymous Is Seriously Scary

> I found an article from March 1st. The media was so busy talking about the Inokashira incident that it got lost, but here it is.

"Patient at Musashino Medical Escapes, Whereabouts Still Unknown"

At around 11:00 PM on February 29th, staff at Musashino Medical General Hospital reported that a patient had gone missing. The missing patient was Yuna Miyamae, a resident of the psychiatric ward. The police searched, but have not found her. Since her clothes were still in her room, it is believed she left wearing a medical gown.

268: Anonymous Is Seriously Scary

> Wow, I seriously didn't see that.

269: Anonymous Is Seriously Scary

> I found her name on the Inokashira victims list, too.

270: Anonymous Is Seriously Scary

> Then she ran from the hospital and killed herself at Inokashira Park? Did she go straight there, or meet with someone first? If you could track where she went, wouldn't they be able to prove whether or not there was group hypnosis?

271: Anonymous Is Seriously Scary

> Yuna...rest in peace.

272: Anonymous Is Seriously Scary

> Was there time for this girl to be hypnotized? I mean, she walked from the hospital to Inokashira, right? There just wasn't enough time for her to sit around and be hypnotized.

273: Anonymous Is Seriously Scary

It was friggin' cold out, and the middle of the night, and she was a hospital patient (even if it was just in the psych ward). On top of that, she walked a long way in a hospital gown. She'd be in pretty weak shape, right? Wouldn't that just make her easier to hypnotize?

274: Anonymous Is Seriously Scary

She clearly left the hospital to go die. Then maybe if we looked at her phone, we could figure out who she was in touch with?

275: Anonymous Is Seriously Scary

So it took six months, but the curse of Kokkuri-san finally got her, huh? Maybe what all the victims of the 256 Incident have in common is that they all played "Kokkuri-san" at least once in the past.

276: Anonymous Is Seriously Scary

>>275

If that's what they had in common, 256 is a pretty realistic number.

277: Anonymous Is Seriously Scary

>>275

Huh? I played Kokkuri-san when I was in middle school, and I'm still alive.

"Man Livestreams One-Man Hide-and-Seek, Never Comes Back"

311: Anonymous FOUND YOU

Hey, remember how the One-Man Hide-and-Seek guy had a sister? The one who said her brother had gone missing and she was looking for him. On the 29th she made a weird tweet.
twitter.cam/+si+sakaue+/status/551912348423900229

312: Anonymous FOUND YOU

>>311

Huh? What's this?

313: Anonymous FOUND YOU

>>311

This is some bad juju.

314: Anonymous FOUND YOU

>>311

I got goosebumps. CALL THE COPS!

315: Anonymous FOUND YOU

>>311

So...what does this mean?

316: Anonymous FOUND YOU

>>311

Come on, there's no way that's true. It's just a coincidence.

317: Anonymous FOUND YOU

>>311

Scary Scary Scary Scary Scary Scary Scary

318: Anonymous Found You

>>311

They...found him? But if that's the place, it doesn't look good.

I wondered what kind of tweet could freak the Basariters out so much, so I clicked the link to go to the Twitter account.

The account belonged to the older sister of the man who'd gone missing during One-Man Hide-and-Seek, it said, and it had been in the *J-CAST* article on the guy, too. For some reason, I felt a little uneasy.

The tweet in question was displayed on the page.

@+si+sakaue+

> Thanks to all of your information, I figured out how to check the location data from the phone. I used it to locate my brother, but the location is really strange, and I think someone might be playing a prank on me.

@+si+sakaue+

> Huh? Huh? What is this? What is this? What is this?
> This doesn't make sense.

@+si+sakaue+

> I'm scared. I'm scared. I'm scared. I'm scared. I'm scared. I'm scared. I'm scared. I'm scared. I'm scared. I'm scared. I'm scared. I'm scared. I'm scared. I'm scared. I'm scared. I'm scared. I'm scared. I'm scared. I'm scared.

@+si+sakaue+

> Someone help me! The location data for my brother's phone doesn't make any sense!
> Ples hlp me!

@+si+sakaue+

> If this is a prank, then stop it! Is this some kind of computer error or something?

@+si+sakaue+

> I'm sorry. I'm really sorry.
> I don't understand.

@+si+sakaue+

> Can someone out there help me with this?
> This is a screenshot of the GPS (?) data from my brother's phone!

I clicked the link.

Tokyo, Mitaka City—

Inokashira Park—

The middle of—

"INOKASHIRA LAKE?!" I gasped as I looked at the screenshot. "Wait, are you serious?"

If this was right, on the night of the 29th, the man who'd vanished during One-Man Hide-and-Seek had sunk to the bottom of Inokashira Lake. And the high school girl who'd been hospitalized after playing Kokkuri-san had died there as well. Two of the victims of occult incidents in Kichijoji were included among the 256.

Which meant...

"There's a good chance the other people I talked about on my site are dead as well!" I got so excited I yelled.

Master Izumin jerked a little, then glared at me with a smile. Both Ryotasu and Myu-Pom, who'd been making small talk, looked shocked.

Still, I couldn't help but shout. "This is a huge scoop! If I write about this on Kirikiri Basara, I'll get billions of hits! Kirikiri Basara will be the only site that can find the truth about the 256 Incident! I won't have to get a job!" In that instant, I forgot all about everything bad that was happening to me, and enjoyed my declaration of victory.

PARANORMAL SCIENCE NVL
Occultic;Nine
オカルティック・ナイン
THERE IS NO SUCH THING AS THE "OCCULT." IT CAN ALL BE DISPROVED BY SCIENCE.
ONLY THOSE WHO HAVE ACCEPTED EVERYTHING
HAVE THE RIGHT TO KNOW THE TRUTH.

▸ site 41: Yuta Gamon

By the time I got out of Blue Moon, it was totally dark.

I ignored the way Ryotasu and Myu-Pom were looking at me, and focused my full attention on writing an article on the One-Man Hide-and-Seek and Kokkuri-san victims. When Master Izumin kicked me out, the two of them were long gone.

"Sheesh. And to think they call themselves Basara Girls," I mumbled as I walked out onto the streets at night.

It was the weekend, and the area around the station was pretty busy. I decided to avoid going that way and take the long route home. Like always, I searched for keyholes as I walked. I was searching as hard as I could, but I only found at most one or two keyholes a day. I'd been astonished to find out that if you excluded apartments and houses where people lived, there just weren't that many keyholes out there. It was bad enough that I was thinking of asking for help on Kirikiri Basara... Of course, there was no way I could do that.

"Oh."

Suddenly I came across an abandoned parking area. The chain on the entrance was locked with a padlock. I quickly walked over to the chain, being careful to see that no one was around me. I took out the gold key and went to put it in the padlock. But...

"Another no, huh?" I sighed and went to leave, only to freeze in shock as I turned around.

A cop on a bike was getting closer. And he was looking straight at me. I felt all the blood drain from my body.

Shit! He saw me. He was going to question me. If he did, I was doomed. They'd lock me in an interrogation room for days, and try to make me out to be Dr. Hashigami's killer.

Run! Run! Run! my mind told me. But if I ran away here, I'd only look more suspicious. And so, I froze completely.

The policeman got off his bike and wordlessly approached me. His sharp eyes were peering right into me. I was like a frog being stared at by a snake. I couldn't speak or run. All I could do was look down and try not to meet his gaze.

The officer stopped in front of me. It was all I could do to keep from just collapsing to the ground in despair. He grabbed the chain I'd been fiddling with and shook it violently. The sound of shaking metal echoed through the area.

"What is this about?" the cop said.

I screamed without thinking. "N-n-n-nothing!"

"..." He kept shaking the chain, but eventually gave up and sighed. "Don't waste my time."

"I'm sorry..." I bowed as low as I could, and surprisingly, the officer said nothing else. He just glared at me and then rode off on his bike.

"Th-that was close..." *If he'd searched me, I would've been finished.*

No, now wasn't the time to be relieved. That cop might decide to come back.

My whole mind was filled with thoughts of getting out of there. And so, I started walking down the road in the opposite way the policeman had gone. It was only when I got to the area in front of the station that I relaxed. I wanted to just crouch down right on the ground. I looked around to see where I was.

I was right in front of the big sign in Harmonica Alley. Just like I'd expected, it was packed. Just being around so many people was making me sick. I couldn't stand to be here for more than a few minutes. But when I looked at the Harmonica Alley sign, I remembered something.

They curse people with black magic, supposedly. I heard that unless you bring them the hair of somebody you want to curse, they won't accept your job.

Was it Master Izumin who'd said that?

The owner of the House of Crimson, Aria Kurenaino. Ryotasu had said that she was pretty close to our age, and she was also very pretty. No, at this point it didn't matter if she was pretty or not. Last month, Ryotasu and Myu-Pom had taken a piece of my hair to the House of Crimson. Pretending that I was a jerk who'd cheated on them, they'd paid more than sixty thousand yen to have a curse put on me.

At first, I hadn't believed in curses at all. But come to think of it, hadn't all these bad things been happening to me since the day I'd been cursed? Ryotasu had explained to me that a "devil" that Aria Kurenaino had a contract with was the one who actually did the cursing. I'd run into that devil, or something like it, just a few days ago...or so I thought.

Yeah. That was the night of the twenty-ninth. The same day as the

256 Incident. I'd run into the devil just a few streets away from here.

Huh? Was that a dream or did it really happen? It didn't matter. What mattered was this: What if Aria Kurenaino's curse really had done this to me? Or maybe Aria Kurenaino was behind the whole thing, and she was the one who'd killed Dr. Hashigami, and hypnotized 256 people as part of the Inokashira Park incident.

"Haha, yeah, right!" I forced myself to laugh. If I didn't, I was going to start suspecting everyone of everything. Maybe the recent occult boom was starting to affect me, too.

It wasn't good to just flail around randomly. My priority needed to be finding the keyhole that matched this golden key. Both Ririka Nishizono and Aria Kurenaino seemed suspicious, but now wasn't the time for caution.

After telling myself that and starting to walk forward, my shoulder collided with a man holding a cigarette.

"Damnit kid, that hurt!"

"I-I'm sorry!" I apologized, and then looked at him and shivered.

His hair was in a punch perm, and he was wearing sunglasses at night. I looked closer and saw he was missing his front teeth.

"Where the hell are you looking when you walk? If apologies were good enough, we wouldn't need the cops!"

"I'll look in front of me when I walk. I promise!" That was all I said before I ran down into Sun Road Shopping Street.

I bought some gyudon takeout for dinner, and then went into one of the side streets of Sun Road. Instantly, there were fewer people. I was sick of the crowds, and finally started to feel a little better.

Suddenly, I turned around.

"..."

There was only one person on the street walking the same direction I was. This time, it was a young man in glasses, but I couldn't see his face. And then I felt the headlights of a car coming in front of me and looked back ahead. The car passed by me.

If I walked quick, I could be home in ten minutes. As I walked, I kept looking around for padlocks and keyholes where I might try the gold tooth key.

"..." What was going on?

After about five minutes, something seemed wrong. It wasn't the padlocks. It wasn't that cop, either... It wasn't Ririka Nishizono or Aria Kurenaino. It was something else.

It felt really nasty. Between now and leaving Blue Moon, nothing had happened besides almost being questioned by that police officer and bumping into that scary guy. So why did I feel so bad?

I turned around once more, confused. Once again, it was just the other young man walking in the same direction as me. I turned back forward and shivered.

The young man I just saw walking about thirty meters behind me was wearing glasses.

"It's the same guy from in front of the station..."

I'd been careful to watch for cops and scary men, but I hadn't been thinking about him. He was just some random extra! Why him? What was going on? Was he following me?

I felt something cold run down my back.

No, no, no.

I tried to chase the thought from my mind. It was a coincidence. It was just a coincidence! If you wanted to go northwest from the station, this was the path you'd take.

But I found myself walking faster.

After I'd run into that man at Harmonica Alley, I'd bought takeout at a gyudon place. It was dinnertime, and it had been crowded inside the store. There were two other people in front of me waiting for their takeout. So, I probably spent five minutes or so waiting there. During that time, where had the man behind me been, and what was he doing? He wasn't in the gyudon place with me.

Maybe he was buying food somewhere at a convenience store or fast food place. Maybe it had taken him five minutes or so to get food, just like it had taken me. Did he have a plastic bag or anything in his hands? Had I seen it when I'd turned around? Damn it, I hadn't looked. I wasn't sure if he had or not.

Why hadn't I looked more carefully? I wanted to know. I wanted to turn around again, but wouldn't it be unnatural to turn around three times? If he was tailing me, and he knew I'd caught him—he might attack me right here. He might stab me, just like Dr. Hashigami was stabbed.

I remembered the look on the dead body's face. The color of the blood on the floor. I remembered the color of the blood as it soaked into his clothes. I wanted to scream and run.

But I couldn't. I needed to pretend not to see anything. It wasn't good to make rash decisions. I didn't have any guarantee he was tailing me at all, but it felt like it would be a bad idea to just go home. If I went inside my house, I could probably escape him, but it was also possible that his goal was to find out where I lived. If that was the case, I couldn't let him find out. I might be putting not just myself in danger, but Mom, too.

So, when I got to the intersection in front of me, I quickly turned right. I glanced behind me as I did so.

The man in glasses was still following me. He was walking right under a streetlamp. The light seemed to glint off the rims of his glasses.

And then I got even more confused. I knew the man's face, somehow. I couldn't remember from where. I couldn't remember from when.

When I was running from the scene of Dr. Hashigami's death, I'd passed by a bunch of students at the school. I'd passed by people who weren't students, too.

Where was it? Where had I seen him?! The alarm bells were going off in my mind.

Crap. Crap. Crap. Crap. Crap. Crap. Crap.

I panicked and went even faster. Would the man turn right like I did, or keep going straight? That was what I hoped to find out. If he turned, that meant he was following me. If he didn't, it would just mean I was getting paranoid.

Go straight. Go straight.

I turned back a little as I walked, waiting for the man in glasses to appear. And the man—

—turned right, without the slightest hesitation.

"Aah...!" I almost screamed. I bit down hard on my molars to stop myself.

That settled it. He was following me! He didn't look like a detective. He felt too young. And he was too thin.

Then who was he? The real killer?! Or was he someone who'd seen me fleeing on the day of the murder? Was he planning to blackmail me for money?

I just needed to run. I needed to get out of here. But to where?

Back to the station? There was a police box there. But I couldn't go to the police! If I did, they'd arrest me for Dr. Hashigami's murder! *So, where should I go?*

I smacked my hand against the case on my shoulder. *Say something, Zonko! You're the one who got me into this mess! This happened because I listened to you, so come out again and help me!*

Of course, just like Zonko had said, she wasn't going to talk to me when there were other people around.

Eventually, I came out to Itsukaichi Street. That would mean that since leaving Blue Moon, I had gone north and then back south, zig-zagging across Kichijoji. Home was only a twenty-minute walk away, but I'd already been walking for almost an hour.

If I went left, I could get to Seimei University. Instinctively, I knew I didn't want to go there, so I turned right. That would take me further from home. I'd be heading back towards Blue Moon. But once I got there, I had no idea how I'd escape.

I looked back, and didn't see the man from before. Was this my chance?

I started to run. And then I started to ask myself what I would do next.

I'd been running without thinking, but of course, I didn't have the stamina to run for kilometers at a time. The man would quickly realize that I'd run. At that point, I wouldn't be able to make excuses. He might try to catch me for real.

What do I do? Why did I run? What the hell am I doing? Think, you idiot!

As I ran, almost in tears, the light in front of me turned red. I ran across the crosswalk without stopping. In front of me was Musashino

Hachimangu Shrine.

There was no time to turn back. I went under the torii arch and into the dark shrine grounds. I could hide in this darkness. That was my bet.

Instead of going to the main shrine, I snuck behind one of the smaller shrines and hid there.

It hurt to breathe. It was taking a long time for my breathing to calm down. I put my hand over my mouth to make myself harder to hear, but it didn't seem to be working. Sweat was pouring out from all over. I felt hot. I wanted to rip off my duffel coat and strip down to my T-shirt. I threw the bag I was holding with the gyudon onto the ground, so it wouldn't make any noise.

Was that man still following me?

Did he see me go into the shrine?

If he didn't, I might be okay. But if he did, I was screwed. There was no place to run.

Please don't be following me, I prayed silently.

I closed my eyes, and I waited for the nightmare to end.

...But it was no good.

A lone shadow was standing just under the torii arch at the entrance.

From where I was hiding, I could only make out the silhouette, but it was definitely the man in glasses I'd seen before.

"...!!"

What do I do? I'm screwed! I'm gonna be murdered here at this shrine, and some old guy walking his dog is gonna find me in the morning, and then I'll be in the evening papers. Will my mom cry, I wonder?

And then—

"Don't you think it's stupid that past this point is a sacred space?" The man's voice echoed throughout the quiet grounds.

It was an intelligent voice. There was no irritation, rage, or anything else contained within it.

"Even if, hypothetically, gods were real, do you think they would choose to live in the middle of the city, with all these cars around?" He was calling to someone.

Who was he calling to?

It was obvious. It was me! He knew I was here, and was trying to scare me!

"Why Kirikiri Basara?"

...Huh? What did he just say? What did he just say?!

"Does it come from the mantra of Gundari Myouou, 'On Kirikiri Basara Un Hatta'?"

He...he knew who I was!

"I heard about you from Miyuu Aikawa. I found out that you were at Seimei University on the day my dad died, too."

"...?!" He knew Myu-Pom?! The only one who knew that I was at Seimei Building 10 that day was Ryotasu...

Did Ryotasu tell Myu-Pom? And did Myu-Pom tell him? And did he just say, "my dad"? Was he talking about Dr. Hashigami? My mind couldn't keep up. I couldn't think.

And then I gasped.

I remembered.

I remembered where I saw his face.

—On TV. It was during Dr. Hashigami's funeral. He'd been there.

He was Dr. Hashigami's son...!

"I didn't kill him!" I'd leapt out of the darkness and screamed, without even realizing it.

It was true that I'd seen his body, and that I hadn't told the police, and that I'd ripped out his gold tooth with a pair of pliers. But… But I didn't…

"It wasn't me! I didn't do it!" I felt like I was going to cry. "Believe me! Please, believe me! I didn't…"

The man—Dr. Hashigami's son—didn't move at all. He scoffed a little, his face still cold.

And this is what he said.

"I don't think you did it."

"…Huh?" He didn't…?

"R-really?"

He nodded.

I felt relieved. At the same time, all the energy drained from my body, and I dropped to my knees right there.

Dr. Hashigami's son slowly walked towards me. In the dim light of the streetlamps, I could just barely make out his expression. I looked so pathetic, but he didn't bat an eye.

"You're definitely the admin for Kirikiri Basara, right?"

"A-are you…Dr. Hashigami's son?"

He nodded. "Sarai Hashigami. I've commented on Kirikiri Basara several times," he said.

For a moment, I didn't understand him, but his words bothered me.

I thought a little. Part of me thought that it was a really small world, if Dr. Hashigami's son was commenting on my blog.

I let the name echo in my mind. And then the fog in my mind lifted.

"Sarai... You mean you're THE Sarai?"

Sarai Hashigami nodded a little.

Maybe the bigger surprise was that Sarai's dad was Dr. Hashigami.

"I've read most of your personal information. Yuta Gamon. A second-year student at Seimei High."

"Oh, yes...that's right."

"I'm a student at Seimei U."

"Huh...?!" We went to the same academy? I had no idea he was so close. It was possible that I passed by him on campus without even knowing it.

"I want you to tell me something." Sarai looked me dead in the eye. "Did you see the place where my father died?"

"...I-I..."

"There's no need to lie to me. I don't think for a moment that you're the killer. There's signs that my father was locked in there and tortured for at least a week. That would've been impossible for you, in light of a number of factors."

Huh? Really? Was that just what Sarai thought? Or was that what the police thought?

"But from what I heard from Miyuu Aikawa, you visited my father's lab around 5:00 PM on the twenty-fourth."

I was surprised to find out that Myu-Pom had told Sarai. I felt a little betrayed. And wait, did Myu-Pom actually know Sarai? *The two of them got in a fight on Nico, didn't they?*

"It's not right to blame her. She was actually worried about you."

"I-I see." He always seemed to be reading my mind. It felt like he was making fun of me, and I found it pretty annoying.

"If it's true that you saw the scene, ran, and never called the police,

I find your actions inexplicable and upsetting, but..."

"..." I couldn't say anything.

Of course I couldn't.

"So, did you see where my father died or not?"

I gulped, and slowly nodded. "I...did."

Sarai didn't move an eyebrow. "If there's anything that bothered you, please tell me."

"Huh? Anything...?"

"Anything. The police aren't giving me much information, so I barely know anything about my father's death." Sarai grabbed me by the shoulders and got closer. "So tell me. What did you see there? If anything seemed strange, tell me, no matter what it is."

Part of me wanted to tell him that this wasn't how you asked people for help, but when I saw his expression, I couldn't. There was nothing in his face that made me think he viewed me as an enemy. If anything, he seemed to be looking to me for help.

Of course he would... His father had been horribly murdered, and the killer hadn't been caught.

Still... *Things that seemed strange, huh?*

The whole thing was so bizarre that I didn't even know where to begin.

The biggest thing that I remembered was—the gold tooth key in my pocket. But there was no *way* I could tell Sarai about that. I mean, what was I supposed to tell him? *I ripped out your dad's gold tooth with a pair of pliers, and I'm still carrying it around with me?*

"...CODE." So the word that came out of my mouth was his father's dying message.

"What did you say? Code?"

"Your father wrote letters on the floor, in his own blood. In English. C, O, D, E."

Sarai gasped and took his hands off me.

"You're telling me there was a dying message?"

"Y-you didn't know?"

Sarai shook his head. "The police wouldn't tell me anything."

Why wouldn't they tell him?

"CODE… I've seen that somewhere…" Sarai put his fingers to his temples and closed his eyes, lost in thought. "At home…in the study? I think I saw a document that said that, a long time ago…"

The study in Sarai's home. That would be Dr. Hashigami's study.

I reflexively put my hand into my pocket and grabbed the gold tooth key within. If there was a lock that this key would fit, it would be in Dr. Hashigami's house.

If I went there…

"Let's look. For a clue." The words came out of my mouth without me thinking, and I was a little surprised at them. "For an important hint to find the real killer…!"

And also, a hint that would prove my innocence.

"No, but…" Sarai frowned for a moment, suddenly hesitant.

At this rate, I was going to lose my chance. I grabbed onto Sarai.

"Please! Don't you want to find the real killer?!"

"Of *course* I want to know why my dad was killed! But it's impossible!"

Sarai pushed me away. I tripped and fell to the ground. He was looking down at me. He kept trying to adjust his glasses to calm himself down, but it only showed how frustrated he was. Just like on the net, it didn't take much to set him off.

"Someone ransacked my dad's study the day he was killed."

...Ransacked it? What?

"After carefully analyzing me and my mother's actions that day, I was able to determine that they entered the study between 4:15 and 5:30 PM. That matches up with my dad's time of death almost exactly. It was a carefully planned crime. Of course, they would've taken any evidence."

When I heard that, I felt as if I were on the verge of stepping into an abyss of conspiracies. I felt the presence of some vast, invisible, and unknowable enemy.

I started to shake.

I glanced at the Skysensor bag that was hanging from my shoulder.

You practically asked *for this when you came here!*

Zonko's words from that day echoed in my mind.

Was I supposed to just spend the rest of my life in fear of the police and the real killer? No. No, I didn't want that!

I'm still a high school student! I'm still seventeen! Sure, maybe I planned to never leave my room, but that was so I could be lazy, not because I wanted to live in fear of some unseen enemy.

There was no way I wanted to spend the rest of my life in fear.

"Just because they ransacked your study doesn't mean they took all the evidence!" I stood up and grabbed Sarai. "L-let's just look at it! Take me there! Please!"

"D-don't blame me...! No matter what happens..." Sarai hesitated a moment, feeling a bit overwhelmed, but then he nodded.

"This isn't a video game or an anime, okay?"

▸ site 42: Yuta Gamon

Sarai Hashigami's house was in an expensive area right near Inokashira Park.

Normally, it was quiet, even though it was so close to the station, but thanks to the 256 Incident, it was now filled with people walking the streets.

There were media trucks and vans parked right on the road. Wasn't that a parking violation? Evidently, the media were staking out Inokashira Park even at night. It must've sucked to be them, considering how cold it was.

It had been only ten days or so since Dr. Hashigami's death, so normally, the media would still be staking out his house. Maybe it was good for Sarai's family that the 256 Incident had pulled all of them away.

"Come in." Sarai opened the gate to his house.

The Hashigami residence was a very ordinary one. There was a pine tree in the yard, and a small pond. He'd probably lived here for years. I'd been imagining something more modern and fancy, so I was a little surprised.

The outside light was on. If the light was on, that meant his family was probably home. Was it okay for me to just come over like this? Sarai didn't seem to care, though.

Sarai opened the front door to the house, and we went inside.

There were several pairs of shoes strewn about the front entrance, and the mail and newspapers were piling up. The place didn't seem dirty. It felt like it had only gotten messy recently.

And there was something else that bothered me.

The house was too quiet.

It was so noisy outside, which only made the contrast more stark.

The outside light was on, but there was no sign of anyone in the house.

Maybe the rest of Sarai's family—his mother, perhaps—had already gone to sleep. After what had happened to his dad, there was no way his family could live normally. Maybe his mom was asleep from exhaustion... Maybe.

When I thought about that, the look on Dr. Hashigami's dead face came back to me, and I quickly shook my head.

"This way," Sarai said.

The professor's study was on the second floor. I was still in the process of taking off my shoes, but Sarai had already started walking up the stairs.

He seemed kind of mad at me. Of course he would be. He'd just said I was inexplicable and upsetting. He probably hated me. But still, the person he should hate wasn't me. It was whoever killed his dad.

It was very strange to be with Sarai, the guy from my message board. It was a miracle, actually. Unfortunately, I couldn't see us ever being friends.

My only real friend...was Ryotasu, anyway.

As I quickly took off my shoes, I realized that Sarai was looking down at me from the staircase.

"Wh-what is it...?" I asked.

"You were just thinking that I was the type of person you don't like, weren't you?"

"No, um..."

"Do you know what humans do when they lie? One thing they do is always look away. And what have you been doing? You seem to be looking down towards your lower right. The other thing they do is blink less. An adult male blinks an average of twenty times a minute. That's once every three seconds. It's been thirty seconds since I've started this conversation, but surprisingly, you haven't blinked once. The third thing is that a small film of sweat forms around the bridge of their nose. The low for today is five degrees. At this hour, it's not that low, but it still can't be more than around seven. That's not a temperature where you sweat. And this house doesn't have the heater running at all. It's the same temperature in here as it is outside, and you're sweating. Your body temperature's gone up because of something I've said that's causing you to panic. There's more. Should I continue?"

"N-no, that's okay!"

What a PITA.

What was with this guy? He kept going on and on about crap that didn't matter. And with this huge smirk on his face, too! Did I really need to know all that stuff now? It would be a lot easier if he just said, "You don't like super-smart jackasses like me, do you? Well, I don't like

NEET scum like you." No, I wouldn't want him saying that to my face. If he said it to me on Twitter or something, I could probably come up with a really good comeback. And wait, how long was he going to stand there? *Just go up the stairs already!* At this rate, I'd be stuck in the front hall forever.

Maybe it was because I was complaining to myself like usual, but the panic I'd been feeling a moment ago had started to subside.

As I listened to Sarai's long, boring speech, I suddenly heard a noise that bothered me.

Both Sarai and I were standing still, but I could hear the sound of a creaking floor. At the end of the first floor hallway, there was a door fitted with frosted glass. It was half-open, but the room inside was dark, and I couldn't see what was going on inside. It was probably the living room or something.

I focused towards the spot in the darkness where I'd heard the noise—and saw a white shadow move.

"Uwah!" I screamed a little in surprise.

"Huh?" Sarai looked a little annoyed. I realized that I'd grabbed onto his arm.

"I'm...sorry. But that was..." I rubbed my eyes.

It looked like an old woman in a white kimono...

Was it Sarai's grandmother? But if it was, why didn't she turn the light on?

Was it...a *ghost?!*

"Are you *sure* you're the admin of KiriBasa?" Sarai sounded unsatisfied.

He must not have seen whatever it was I saw.

Okay, I'll just ignore the shadow then. Yeah. People see things all the time. Yup. Later, I could send Special Correspondent Ryotasu on a mission to find out what it was. Then I could write a post about whether it was a ghost or just some old woman.

I followed Sarai up the stairs.

There were three rooms on the second floor. Sarai stopped at the one near the end of the hall.

"Is this Dr. Hashigami's study...?"

"Yup."

The door was shut. There was no way to see what was inside. Sarai had said it had been "ransacked," but...

"I'll wait here. If you want to investigate, do it on your own."

"Huh? Why? Is there a ghost in here too?!"

"A ghost? What are you talking about?"

"Oh, nothing..."

"I still haven't processed my feelings toward my dad. My emotions get in the way no matter what I do."

He didn't have to always put things in such an obnoxious way.

"I-I lost my dad, too..."

"What?"

"So, um..."

I kinda understood how he felt...

"D-don't think...that you're the only one who's got it tough..."

"Ahem..."

Oh, crap. That didn't come out right.

Sarai looked annoyed, but he didn't say anything. He just silently opened the door to the study and nodded.

I bowed and slid past him into the room.

"...It's cleaned up." I was surprised.

He'd said it had been ransacked, so I was imagining something like out of a TV show, but that wasn't the case at all.

His family must have cleaned it up. Most of the books and papers were piled neatly on the floor and tied up with string. The bookcase that covered one of the walls was mostly empty.

There was a simple study desk in the middle of the room. The desktop had been cleaned off, and now had only a lonely-looking pen holder lying on top. It was very different from the desk at his lab, which had been covered in strange objects.

But if things were like this...

"There's no way to find any clues..." What I was after was a clue to who had killed the professor. The ideal thing would be to find the keyhole for the golden tooth key. If I found a clue to the real killer, I'd be able to go tell the police that I was the first one who found the body. I wouldn't have to fear that they'd arrest me instead.

But...

"I guess it's not like in the detective shows, huh?" I said.

But I had to look anyway. My life was on the line, after all. I didn't want my life to end at this age.

I started by looking at the covers of the books on the floor. They were similar to the ones in his room at the school. The occult books and physics books in particular stood out. Then there were old papers, and what looked like drafts of his *Mumuu* column.

I wanted to read them all, but they were tied so tightly that it would be difficult to get the string off. *Maybe I should get permission from Sarai later...*

I didn't see anything besides the books. There weren't any cardboard boxes or anything. Maybe they'd gotten rid of everything.

So the only thing left to check was the desk. I wasn't sure what to do, so I started by trying to open the top of its three drawers—and it suddenly stuck.

The top drawer was locked. I looked closely and saw that there were marks that seemed to have been made with metal along the surface, as if someone had tried to force it open.

"A key..." I gulped.

I put my hand to my chest and took a deep breath.

Calm down.

"This is definitely...worth trying, yeah."

I took a glance at Sarai, who was still waiting outside the room...

...and took the gold tooth key out of my pocket.

That's right. This is what I'd been looking for. How many locks had I tried since that day? And none of them had fit. But I'd realized...

The answer was inside Dr. Hashigami's house. *In other words, right here.*

It was worth coming here after all! Now I could prove my innocence! With a mixture of joy and nervousness, I stuck the gold tooth key into the lock.

I turned it slowly—

"Huh...?"

And it didn't move at all.

Of course. I hadn't wanted to admit it, but the sizes of the key and the keyhole didn't match at all. The key was way too small.

"I guess it was too much to hope for..."

I had gotten my hopes up, which only made it worse. I felt like slamming my forehead into the desk.

"They say truth's stranger than fiction, but that's not true. Miracles don't just happen in the real world."

But still, this drawer was locked. That was a fact.

There must be a clue inside. It was my only hope at this point.

So I couldn't give up.

Once, a long time ago, I'd hidden the ero-doujin I'd bought at Tora no Ara from my mom behind a drawer. By now, I was more careful, and carefully switched them between multiple hiding spots. So because of that, I knew a lot about drawers.

I decided to ignore the locked top drawer, and see what was in the two below it. Both of them were empty.

I took the second and third drawers out of the desk. This made it easier to get at the top one. If I was lucky, I might be able to reach around and grab whatever was in there.

I stuck my head into the empty spot below the drawers and looked up.

"Wh-what the heck?"

The bottom of the first drawer had been destroyed. There was nothing but empty space there.

Someone had tried the same approach, then destroyed the bottom of the drawer and taken whatever was in there.

Whatever the killer had been after must have been in here.

Evidently whoever had ransacked this room had been a lot more careful than I thought.

"I was too late..."

There was nothing left here now.

I sighed.

I was just an amateur. Just a high school student. Just a NEET god. There was no way I could find a clue like a detective in a mystery novel.

After this room had been ransacked, Sarai's family and the police would've searched it thoroughly. So of course, in a sense, this was to be expected.

So why'd I get my hopes up? It was useless. No matter what I did, I wasn't going to find anything. The killer's group wasn't stupid enough to leave behind any evidence that someone like me could find, and the cops weren't idiots.

In the face of this obvious and inevitable result, I just felt exhausted.

I didn't want to move. So much had happened today that I was tired.

I couldn't take any more. I should just go home and hide in my room. And then I could just wait for them to find the real killer. I could just wait and live in fear of the cops coming to visit. I could skip school. I wouldn't be able to graduate, but that didn't matter.

I gave up and just lay down on the floor right there.

It doesn't matter....none of this matters...

I almost cried when the thought came to me. I tried to wipe away the tears and calm myself down.

I found myself looking up at the ceiling. There were lots of little tiny holes.

It was the kind of stuff you saw in the music room at school. I think it was for soundproofing. Or were they tiny holes to let air pass? I couldn't remember seeing them in a house before.

But the holes in a music room ceiling were placed at regular intervals. The ones here were different. Several of them were filled with putty or something. It looked really bad, like something a child had done as a prank.

"To keep the rain from leaking in...?" I wondered. "Nah, no way."

Did they hire a contractor to do this? Like maybe he was supposed to fill all the holes, but stopped halfway through for some reason?

"That ceiling's weird."

I started to count the holes. There was a character in *JoJo* who would calm himself by counting prime numbers. Maybe I could calm myself down that way.

But I quickly started to feel a little sick. My vision was starting to dim.

The dots on the ceiling were lined up in rows, but several of them were filled.

I squinted and saw what looked like a face... Maybe.

Didn't I used to play this game all the time as a kid?

I focused on three random holes and stared at them intently. That was enough. They instantly resolved themselves into the parts of a face—two eyes and a mouth.

"Right, right. This is the so-called simulacra effect. I know," I muttered.

Sarai had given a lecture on it before at Kirikiri Basara.

What a stupid-looking face.

"Hey there, ceiling-chan." I said, jokingly. "Did you see what they took from this room? If you did, can you tell me?'

"The answer's—BZZZTT—right in front of you!—ZZZzZZ—How come you can't see it? Are you stupid?"

"Uwah!" I leaped up onto my feet.

I was hearing a voice. That was impossible...

"A-a talking ceiling?!"

And it was a girl's voice, too! I was the only one in this room. Unless Sarai was outside with a voice changer, there was no reason I should be hearing a girl's voice.

"Ceilings don't talk—ZZZzZZTT—you idiot."

"..."

Wait a second. Wait just a second.

This slightly muffled, bratty voice...

"Zonko?! You scared me. I'm hearing a lot of static for some reason." I opened the case to the Skysensor. The power was off. "But why did you decide to start talking now?"

"I don't—ZZZzzz—have time to talk about it."

"Huh? Not again."

"The old ghost—zzzzz—lady is—Zzzz—gonna come to this room soon."

"Ghost?" When she said that, I felt a cold shiver run down my back.

That thing I'd seen downstairs that looked like an old woman in a white kimono. Was that really...?

"Well—ZZZZ—I'm joking about her being—zz—a ghost."

"You're joking?"

Huh? What? What's going on?

It felt like the static was getting worse.

"That old lady is—zzzZZZ—that four-eyes'—zzz—mom."

His mom was an old lady?

"What are you talking about?"

"All the stress must've aged her that badly. BZzzz—but that's a sign of how scared—zzz—she is of other people. She might think—ZZzzz—that you're a thug—zzz—who's come to raid this room."

"I got permission from Sarai—"

"There's no time to explain that—zzzzZZZZZzz—listen carefully.

You can pretend to be a detective, but in that world—zzzz—in the real world—zzz—you won't find anything."

"Wh-what are you trying to say? Do you know what it is I'm looking for?"

No. That wasn't it.

"You know what was hidden in this room, don't you?!" "You're already a part of this—zzzzzzBZZZzz—you can't help it."

"Just explain things. This isn't a movie or a TV show, so instead of giving me hints, give me the answer!"

"I just told you. The answer is—zzzZZ—that ceiling—zzzzzZZZZ—that you're staring at."

"That doesn't tell me anything!"

All those holes on the ceiling—

Irregular dots—

A soundproofed ceiling for a music room—

A failed attempt at fixing rain leaks—

A kid's prank, filling them with putty—

Putty?

Suddenly I found myself looking at the lonely pen holder on the desk. I'd been ignoring it until a moment ago, but for some reason I was noticing it now. It was filled with red and black pencils—and a tube of putty.

"Is this ceiling..."

It wasn't a half-assed repair job? In other words, the professor himself, not a contractor, had done this.

Which meant that the holes were filled deliberately!

"Zonko! Some of the holes are filled up! Do you mean this is a message the professor left?"

"You're actually smart—zzzzzBBBZZzzzz—for once today. It's—zzzzzz—code."

"Code? CODE again? You mean these rows of dots?"

"Figure out the rest for yoursel—zzzBZZZZ—don't poya-poya—zzzzz—the old woman—ghost is—BZzzzBZzzz—"

"Hey, wait!"

"Bzzzzzzzzzzzz-" The voice disappeared, leaving only static.

"Zonko!"

What the hell was going on here? She just showed up, talked for a while, gave me a bunch of orders, and then disappeared without answering any of my questions! The room fell silent again.

I listened for a while, but I didn't hear Zonko.

I looked back up at the ceiling.

There was no way I could solve this.

"I'm not even a detective," I muttered. What had the professor meant when he'd left CODE as a dying message?

What kind of elaborate message did he need to hide with those letters…?

"Hmm?"

In other words, "CODE" meant…

Something encrypted to dots…

"Are these letters?"

"—zzzz—Not—zzz—bad!"

"Wait, you're still here?!"

PARANORMAL SCIENCE NVL
Occultic;Nine
オカルティック・ナイン
THERE IS NO SUCH THING AS THE "OCCULT." IT CAN ALL BE DISPROVED BY SCIENCE.
ONLY THOSE WHO HAVE ACCEPTED EVERYTHING
HAVE THE RIGHT TO KNOW THE TRUTH.

"For us, the spirit world has long left the realm of fantasy." Takasu's dramatic voice drew the gazes of the seated men. "There is no difference, strictly speaking, between the spirit world and our own real world. This was proven by Nikola Tesla a century ago."

Takasu paused for a moment and squinted into the darkness at the back of the room.

"...Our leader has told us that in this world, we exist alongside the will of the dead. We use the common phrase 'spirit world,' but it does not refer to another world. It's the same as this world, and it always has been. In terms of quantum mechanics, the spirit world and the real world 'overlap,' the one difference being that that in one, time does not flow."

That difference had been their biggest barrier.

"Go to the spirit world and you'll find yourself trapped in a 'Prison of Time.' Solving that problem has been our last and greatest task."

At the end of their research, Takasu and the others had reached the "prison of time." In that prison, real time expanded, and escape was presently impossible.

"If it weren't for that prison, we would've chosen death a long time ago," Hatoyama said bitterly.

Takasu nodded. "But at last, we have a hint to help us solve the problem."

Takasu displayed digitized text on his tablet. It was an unpublished paper they'd recovered just a few days ago from Isayuki Hashigami's study, entitled "Time and the Spiritualizing World."

Finding this was what had made possible Takasu's decision to abandon the entire first generation.

"Both myself and the RIKEN team read the report, and it was very interesting. If this were to be made public, it would overturn everything humanity thought it knew. Of course, it doesn't contain all the answers, but if we use this to reorient our research team's priorities, we may be able to synchronize time between the spirit world and the real one. And what that makes possible, is—" Takasu spoke once again in a dramatic voice as he looked around at the seated men.

"The acquisition of the spirit world."

▸ site 44: Shun Moritsuka

"A molar, a doujin manga, a fortune-teller, and black magic, huh... Kichijoji's turning into a fantasy world that would surprise even Conan these days."

I'd been following Yuta Gamon for about fifteen minutes.

He was wearing a yellow and grey duffel coat that made him easy to spot, and he'd been glancing left and right the entire time he walked. Even if he was scared, he was still moving fast. He'd hurried all the way here.

But it didn't seem like he'd noticed me.

"Well, even with these fantasy mysteries going around, my first card I should draw for this stage...is Kirikiri Basara."

Yuta Gamon went into Kichijoji Park.

It was an unobtrusive park in the middle of a residential area. It barely got any visitors to begin with. Only the locals knew there was a park there at all.

But today, there was someone waiting for him.

A young girl with big boobs. She was...cute, but looked stupid.

Maybe there weren't any girls in the real world who had that combination of brains and voluptuousness Mine Fujiko had.

Once he met up with the girl, they left the park and started walking to Kichijoji Theater.

There were love hotels down there...

"...But I guess he wouldn't be up for that right now, huh?" I slyly muttered.

Sleeping with a girl was probably the *last* thing on the mind of the person I was tailing.

He was a suspect in Isayuki Hashigami's murder, after all. He was probably terrified that the police might come knocking on his door at any minute.

In fact, I was sure of it.

If I took his fingerprints and compared them with the ones that were left all over Dr. Hashigami's seminar room, they'd match.

If that happened, the cops would arrest him, and announce his capture at a press conference.

And then the case would, at least on the surface, be closed.

On the surface.

"It would be easy to arrest him, but...I want an opponent I can chase constantly, one where an invisible bond of trust develops even though we're detective and thief, you know?"

If nothing else, the boy I was chasing wasn't the sort. He wasn't the type I wanted to chase.

"I'd run after him, waving a pair of handcuffs and screaming, 'Stop!' and he'd say, 'No way!' That's the kind of guy I'm looking for."

Well, even if I wasn't going to find anybody like that, tailing someone was still fun.

The two people I was following went inside a shady-looking café on the second floor of a multiuse building.

I could see the name of the café at the bottom of the stairs.

Café☆Blue Moon.

Seemed it sold alcohol at night.

"Hmm... That's a pretty grown-up date for a modern teenage couple. I thought kids with no money and lots of time either went to McDonald's, or played with their phones like idiots in freezing cold at Inokashira Park."

Or maybe...there was some reason they had to come here?

"No way. Hahaha."

I decided to go in, too.

It didn't look like a place that would get a lot of customers, so there was a chance I'd run into my target.

But if that happened, I'd figure something out.

Just as I put my foot on the stairs, my phone rang. I wasn't sure if that was good timing or bad.

"Yes. This is Agent Moritsuka."

"Why aren't you following the 256 incident?" the person on the phone asked.

"That's a stupid question. Do you want me to dance with the ghost of Nikola Tesla? Either way, the 'list' will connect to the 256."

"So you're telling me the key is Isayuki Hashigami, after all?"

"It's the only way to catch the ghost by the tail. There's a meaning to the number 256. And Isayuki Hashigami knew what that meaning was," I said as I walked up the stairs to Blue Moon.

PARANORMAL SCIENCE NVL
Occultic;Nine
オカルティック・ナイン
THERE IS NO SUCH THING AS THE "OCCULT." IT CAN ALL BE DISPROVED BY SCIENCE.
ONLY THOSE WHO HAVE ACCEPTED EVERYTHING
HAVE THE RIGHT TO KNOW THE TRUTH.

▸ site 45: Yuta Gamon

"Oh, you're finally here... hmm?" I looked towards the entrance of the room expecting to see Sarai, but instead I saw a small middle school boy that I'd never seen before.

He was wearing a trench coat, but it was clearly much too big for him. It looked a lot like cosplay.

Wait—*was* it cosplay? It didn't seem right to stare, but I couldn't help myself.

Was he really in middle school? He looked shorter than me, but his face didn't look as young as I'd expected.

Maybe... Maybe the police had chosen a detective who didn't look like a professional and sent him after me? There was still no sign that the police were going to visit me over Dr. Hashigami's murder, but every day, I imagined them getting closer and closer.

Thanks to the 256 Incident, there had been cops everywhere in Kichijoji over the last few days, and I passed by them quite a bit. Honestly, it was bad for my heart.

"Sarai-kyun's late, huh?" Ryotasu stifled a yawn, completely oblivious to my troubles.

Last night, I'd visited Sarai's house and found out that there were letters hidden on the ceiling of his study. It seemed to me like the professor's word, "CODE," was referring to those encrypted letters. Although honestly, it had been mostly Zonko who'd told me that. But I had no idea how to actually turn the dots into letters. After I told Sarai, he'd contacted me this morning and told me he'd solved the "CODE" riddle. It had been less than a day.

He had personality issues, but he was a genius. No, maybe his personality was weird *because* he was a genius. He was smarter in person than he was online.

So we'd promised to meet at Blue Moon, but he'd said some crap about coming after work.

This was so important, and there was so little time. Why did he care so much about his damn job? Was this his way of being a dick to me? Whose board did he think he was commenting on all the time?

I went to take a sip of the water in front of me when I felt a cold wind and shivered.

The cosplaying middle school boy was still standing with the entrance door open, and the cold air was blowing in.

"Hey, boyfriend! It's cold out. Can you shut the door?" Master Izumin said from behind the counter, turning towards the door. But when he saw that the person there wasn't someone he recognized, he put his hands over his mouth.

"Oh wow, a new customer? Sorry, I didn't realize."

"Are you not open yet?"

"We most certainly are! It's not night so I can't serve alcohol, but of course we're open! Though sometimes we do get visitors who aren't *really* customers. Hehehe." Master Izumin glanced at me with a creepy smile.

I'll admit I only ever order water here. I thought about saying something, but I didn't want to get into an argument over something so stupid now, so I just ignored it.

More importantly—

"Then give me whatever you recommend. Something cold."

"Sure thing. Sit wherever you like."

The cosplaying middle school boy came into the shop and sat a ways off from me.

Our eyes met and he flashed me the innocent smile of a child.

It felt strange.

Until now, I'd had Blue Moon basically to myself in the afternoon, so it was rare to see another customer.

From the way Master Izumin was acting, this was his first time at the café. Was he really just a customer? Or maybe—

"Here you go! 'Today's Fully Loaded Lucky Latte, Supervised by Miyuu Aikawa.'"

Wait, he served him THAT?

He called it a latte, but it looked like a muddy grey soup. Like cement before it dried.

And he said Myu-Pom supervised it, but that was a total lie.

The cosplaying middle school boy was reacting with exaggerated joy, oblivious to the hell that was to come. If he drank it down and liked it, like Ryotasu did, it would mean he was a hell of a lot more than he appeared.

"Wow, this is amazing. It looks like it packs a punch!"

Without the slightest doubt in his voice, he put the straw to his mouth and took a sip—

"Huh? He's drinking it normally..."

And then started to hack and cough.

"GWAAHH! This is barf! This is total barf! What the hell is this?"

"Pffft..." I laughed to myself.

Evidently, he was just a dork. *Somebody give me back the HP I lost when he came in.*

And then he handed me the terror-drink.

"You're laughing, but you'll understand when you drink it! Try it! It's terrible!"

"No... No thanks. I can guess just from the way it looks, and I know that series of drinks."

More importantly, the way he'd said "barf" was striking me as increasingly funny, and it hurt not to laugh.

"I want to try it..." Ryotasu was sitting next to me, looking at the drink with stars in her eyes. She looked like she could reach out and grab the glass at any moment.

"Ryotasu, that's amazing... He says it's barf...and you *still* want to drink it?"

"Hmph." Master Izumin was pouting and looking upset. "I put all the lucky items for today in it! It's rude to say it doesn't taste good! Hmph! HMPH!"

"Sir, even if you put in all lucky ingredients, this taste is definitely unlucky!" The cosplaying middle school boy was laughing, but he was being utterly brutal towards Master Izumin.

Not bad.

Master Izumin had a very forceful appearance and personality, and it took guts to be able to talk to him like that just five minutes after meeting him.

"Still, I didn't know that there were barf-drinks like this in the world."

"Feel free to try the whole Barf Series." I was starting to lose the ability to not laugh, so I interrupted them.

I'd held back my laughter so much my stomach hurt.

The cosplaying middle school boy was still going on.

"I guess if you wanted to give the series a name, you could call it 'The Barf-Drinks.' Or maybe not. Maybe something more dreamy, like 'Fantastic Barf'? No... Or if the theme is 'luck,' maybe just..."

"Lucky Barf!" Ryotasu's idea, unsurprisingly, was the worst one of all. That was something different entirely. Who'd want to drink that?

"Mask of Barf!"

That one sounded too much like Zorro.

"Barf-Barf!"

That wasn't right at all.

"Aww, jeez! What is wrong with you people! Gamota! I'm going upstairs! As punishment, you watch the store! I'm out of tequila! Sheesh!"

It didn't feel quite fair to make me do it, but Master Izumin left the store, shoulders shaking with anger. There was a small café/bar on the floor upstairs, run by a different owner. That one wasn't open during the day, so I'd never been there.

"I'll go too!"

Ryotasu followed Master Izumin, and it was just me and the cosplaying middle school boy, and we were still laughing.

I laughed so much all the dark emotions I'd felt over the last week disappeared.

It felt like it had been a long, long time.

And for that, I needed to thank him.

He offered me the fully loaded lucky drink once more.

"Here, you should take a drink. Just a sip."

"No way." I knew it tasted like barf. I wasn't going to drink it.

We'd been repeating that same exchange for a while now, and it was still funny. At this point, everything we said seemed funny.

"You know, you look just like Zenigata, man. If that's cosplay, it's barf-inducing."

"Cosplay, huh? That's my barf-dream."

"Sometimes you get girls who are barfy-cute at cosplay conventions. I keep trying to get Ryotasu to do it."

"I've been to Comiket. I bought some barfy doujin."

"What's a barfy doujin? Ahahah. I don't think I want to know, do I?"

"By the way, it's barfy-hot in here. Aren't you hot in that?"

"I'm barfy-fine."

"I hear if someone rips out your molar, it barfy-hurts."

"Barfff—?!"

What?

What did he just say?

"By the way, this isn't cosplay. This is my uniform." The cosplaying middle school boy was still laughing as he took what looked like a notebook out of his jacket pocket and showed it to me. It was something I'd only ever seen on police shows on TV.

A police badge...

"You were just thinking that you're in barfy-trouble, weren't you? So, I'll ask again. Have you ever pulled out someone's molar?"

"Th-the police..." I'd let my guard down!

Hahhahh hahh...

I'd let my guard down...!

I could barely breathe.

"Had I ever pulled out a molar?" He knew everything! He wasn't a middle-schooler! He wasn't a cosplayer! He was a real detective, just like I'd first thought! I'd been fooled by his appearance! I'd been an idiot to open up to him!

"Oh? Are we done with the barf stuff? Because you look like you're about to barf. What's wrong, Yuta Gamon, Student Number 3 in Class 2-B at Seimei High?"

"...!"

He was here to arrest me!

My teeth started to chatter. I bit down on my molars to make them stop.

This was bad. This was really bad. Sarai wasn't here yet. Sarai wasn't here to testify to my innocence! Even though I was here alone with a detective! Why had Master Izumin and Ryotasu and Myu-Pom and Sarai all left me alone?! *Someone, anyone, come and help me!* At this rate, I'd be arrested! I'd be taken to the police station and it would be over! They'd lock me in a room and interrogate me, alternating between feeding me katsudon and cussing me out in some cliche good-cop bad-cop routine until I confessed to a crime I didn't commit!

I needed to escape somehow.

But—

Then I realized.

I'd thought that this detective had come here alone. But did he, really?

What if there were a bunch of tough-looking detectives outside, waiting for me? Maybe there were dozens of cop cars lined up on the street outside. When that idea flashed through my mind, I couldn't move another step.

"It wasn't…me…"

"What are you talking about?"

"It wasn't me…!"

"This conversation's turning barfy. I just asked if you'd ever pulled a molar out. I'm going to a dentist to get my wisdom teeth removed. And I bet it hurts like barf. I've always hated dentists…"

He was lying. Wisdom teeth, my ass. He was laughing the whole time, but his eyes weren't laughing at all.

"So if you've ever pulled out a molar, I'd like you to tell me how it went. I mean, you and I are barf-brothers, right? Hahaha."

There was no way I could laugh.

Sweat was pouring out of my body.

I couldn't breathe. If I breathed, it felt like he'd accuse me.

I looked frantically for an exit, but I couldn't think.

All I could do was retreat into a world of fantasy and think about how nice it would be if I could teleport.

Just when I was about to give up—

"I'm back, Gamotan! Ryotasu went with me, so I got a little present! Look at this delicious chiffon cake!"

Ryotasu and Master Izumin were back.

At the same time they came in, the detective put a rumpled 1000-yen bill on the table and stood up.

"!!" I gasped.

"Anyway, I have to get going."

"...?"

Going? Where? I couldn't look at his face. All I could do was stare at my feet and pray that nothing happened, and that he didn't take me away.

"Oh, what's wrong, Gamota-kun? You're soaking with sweat," asked Master Izumin.

"Pu-♪ u-♪ ru? Pu-♪ u-♪ ru? Pu-♪ u-♪ ru-♪ da-♪ pu-♪ u-♪ ru?" Ryotasu was singing the Puuru Song, or perhaps the Pool Song, as she danced.

But of course, I couldn't join in.

"I'm glad I got to have a barfy-chat with you today."

"..."

The detective headed for the exit.

He wasn't going to arrest me? Why not?

"Sir, I've left the money for the barfy-latte on the table."

"Stop calling it 'barfy'! I've never had someone insult my drinks like that. It hurts."

"Hahaha. Sorry. I'm an honest person." The detective laughed in a loud voice.

He turned back to me and waved a little.

"See you again," he said, and he left.

He really left.

I waited over ten minutes, and he never came back.

"Am I...safe...? Or did he let me go...?"

"Poya-ya?" Ryotasu tilted her head and made a noise like an idiot. But I'd never been so happy to see her empty-headed face before.

I finally stopped feeling nervous, and suddenly felt very tired.

What was that detective thinking?

"But still..."

That strange way he talked, like he was making fun of you, and the way he tried to trick you into saying things... I thought I'd heard it somewhere before.

Yeah, somewhere...

"Myu-Pom's Niconico Live Fortune-Telling?!"

▸ site 46: Aria Kurenaino

It felt a little awkward being in Harmonica Alley in the afternoon.

I lived a nocturnal life, like a vampire, and it was rare for me to be in the shop at this hour. A life lived without sunlight suited my biorhythms far better.

But today I'd been summoned here at this hour. Thanks to that, I felt a bit sleep-deprived. My mind felt hazy.

The window was covered with a black curtain, and a little bit of light leaked through. The countless particles of dust that filled the air of the store glistened in it. As I followed the dust with my eyes, I started to feel like I was drunk. I poured some steaming herbal tea into my favorite cup to stop from throwing up.

"So," I said to the empty shop, "did you find a clue?"

The only one who could call me here was the devil.

I'd sensed him the minute I'd come into the shop, but I hadn't spoken to him yet.

There was no explanation as to why he'd summoned me here. Maybe he'd called me here now because I would be too busy at night?

Impossible, I thought.

The devil wouldn't care about that, and I didn't expect him to.

I was just here because he'd told me to come.

There was nothing more to it than that.

〈Yeah, I caught 'em. Just now, actually.〉 The devil's unpleasant voice echoed in my head.

I never got used to hearing it, but still, I felt relieved. It made me feel like I was still connected to him.

The unpleasant voice was a small price to pay for a contract with a devil.

〈You remember that guy in the trench coat who was watching this place?〉

"...?"

Watching this place...? When was that?

As I tried to remember, I could sense the devil clicking his tongue in frustration.

〈You're not careful. That's why you get set up.〉 "I make sure to forget anything I'm not interested in."

Of course, the devil had a point.

Whoever had put Dr. Hashigami's hair into my mailbox had known that I was careless like that.

I just wanted to live life like a dead girl, possessed by a devil. That was all.

〈A guy who looks like a little kid, wearing a trench coat and a cap. I've seen him at least twice wandering around outside.〉

"Who is he?"

〈No idea. But it's clear he's planning something. So, last time I saw him, I decided to follow him instead. And then I ran into an unexpected group.〉

An unexpected group?

〈You remember those two girls who asked for the Devil's Ritual?〉 I did. They'd asked me to curse a boy who'd been cheating on them. They were still in high school, but paid almost seventy thousand yen like it was nothing. I'd wondered why they didn't seem to be that upset when they were willing to pay that much money.

The boy they'd had cursed… His name was Yuta Gamon, if I remembered correctly.

〈I followed the guy in the trench coat and ran into one of them. The bitch with the huge tits.〉

"That's a disgusting way to describe her."

〈And that ain't all. The manwhore she told you to curse was there, too.〉

"…"

〈The client, the guy she wanted to curse, and the shady asshole who's been hanging around out front were all in the same place. It's a place called Café☆Blue Moon.〉

"Sure it's not a coincidence?"

〈I'm telling you, stupid. There was nobody else in the place. The three of them were talking about something. It looked weirdly serious. It's obvious they're all working together to investigate us.〉

"If they're trying to find out about the existence of devils…" I took "Coven," one of my dolls, and pressed down hard on each of its five eyes, "we'll have to respond appropriately."

If anyone found out I had a contract with a devil, my peaceful life would be over, and more rats would start to try to sniff around in my past.

I did not want that.

⟨If they want a fight, let's give one to them first.⟩

"..."

I took another sip of herbal tea to calm myself down—

And realized it had gone cold.

▸ site 47: Sarai Hashigami

The sun was about to set, and the sky was starting to turn purple.

When I opened the door to Café☆Blue Moon, where I was supposed to meet Yuta Gamon, it was already past five.

It was my first time in the place. The interior design seemed very adult. Not the kind of place a high schooler would choose. Between the decorations and the faint smell of tar, it was less like a café and more like a café bar.

I came up with several hypotheses about the connection between Yuta Gamon and this place, but I decided it was a waste to spend valuable brain memory on something like that and gave up halfway.

There were three other people in the room, besides the owner.

A man and two women.

The man was Yuta Gamon. He was sitting in a corner seat, and had his hands wrapped around his knees for some reason.

One of the girls was Miyuu Aikawa. I'd met her earlier. She was the one who'd told me about Yuta Gamon.

When our eyes met, she looked surprised, then stood up and gave me a little bow. I nodded to her.

As for the other girl…

I didn't know her, and yet…

"Poor Sarai-kyun! ♪ Poor Sarai-kyun! ♪"

P-poor Sarai-kyun?!

For some reason, this woman sympathizing with me was sitting next to Yuta Gamon, so I figured she was with him, but…

Now she was dancing around the shop. Looking at her, I lost all confidence in my analysis. That's how hard it was to read her actions.

I wasn't sure if she was part of Kirikiri Basara, or maybe she was just an employee here at Blue Moon. That would only make sense if the place included a service where the employees danced for the customers, though.

…It was immediately clear, however, that this wasn't that type of place.

If she was taking pity on me, that meant she knew my dad was dead. But that didn't tell me who she was.

As for Yuta Gamon, he was glaring at me angrily.

"What is it? I'm sorry I'm late, but I'd already been scheduled to work, and I told you that over the phone."

"…"

Gamon said nothing. Instead, he just pouted and looked away. He was acting just like a child, but—

"You look pale. Something bad happened because I was late, didn't it? But I wasn't the direct cause of whatever it was, so you can't bring yourself to blame me. Is that it? Did the police question you or something?"

Gamon's whole body twitched.

"H-how..."

"It's obvious."

Holding your knees, psychologically speaking, means you're trying to protect yourself. At least, that's what one theory says. It's the same thing pill bugs do.

In other words, despite the fact that Gamon was waiting at the place he'd specified, he was so afraid he felt the need to protect himself. And Gamon's biggest fear was that he'd be arrested for Isayuki Hashigami's murder. The only reason he'd agreed to meet me here, knowing that he might run into the police, was that he wanted proof of his innocence—in other words, a clue to the real killer.

Which meant he'd made a bad call. On his way here, or perhaps while he was waiting, someone from the police had made contact with him.

"That detective knew me. It wasn't a coincidence. He was here because he was after me. But for some reason, he didn't arrest me. Either he let me go, or he's hoping I'll lead him to something."

"..."

Evidently he hadn't been asked to go to the station.

It was quite possible.

Just like I'd decided Gamon wasn't the killer, the police—or perhaps only part of the investigative team—might have reached the same conclusion.

It was still strange that they didn't even question him, though.

"Um, what's this about a detective?" Aikawa seemed confused.

"Huh? Um... No, we're just talking about how there's so many police officers around Kichijoji lately."

From the terrible excuse he was giving her, it didn't look like

Gamon had told her about his witnessing my father's murder.

He probably wanted to change the subject, because he turned to me.

"A-anyway, tell me about the CODE riddle that was hidden on the ceiling."

That's right. That was why I came here today.

"Hey, if there's four of you here, can you at least order something? Gamota never orders anything but water!" The bartender, a very heavily muscled man, was twisting his body back and forth as he spoke. It was pretty disgusting.

"F-forget it! The mystery! Tell me already!" Gamon sounded irritated.

"Fine. I'll get started."

Me, Aikawa, and the girl who'd started dancing—she said her name was Narusawa—each ordered something. Then I put a piece of paper on the table. Gamon and the rest all looked at it.

It was a photo of all the holes in the ceiling of my father's study. Gamon had taken it yesterday.

Just like he'd said, there was a message from my dad there.

I'd succeeded in decoding it last night. It would've been incredibly difficult to solve this mystery from scratch. But once you knew that it was rows of letters, it wasn't that hard at all. This was my father's dying message.

I'd only waited to tell Gamon this morning because I'd forgotten.

"Boards with all these holes like the ones on the ceiling are called pegboards. You've seen them used on the walls in music rooms, I'm sure."

"They block sound, right?"

I shook my head in answer to Aikawa's question. "They don't block sound. They absorb it. They reduce the rate at which sound emitted in the rooms is reflected, and allow a sound-absorbing material behind the pegboard to absorb it."

"Huh? Then those holes don't exist to shut out sound from the outside?"

"They might work to do that a little, but that's not their real purpose."

"Wait, isn't it actually really rare to use something like this in a house?" Gamon's eyebrows furrowed as he spoke.

"Yeah. My dad wasn't a musician or anything. There was no sense in using a pegboard in the study. This one was put in when he did a sudden remodeling of the study a year ago. He didn't remodel anything else in the house. When I asked him why at the time, he dodged the question."

Thinking back, that was probably when my dad went from denying the occult to saying it existed.

"Then Dr. Hashigami put that pegboard in to hide a message from the start? Isn't that kind of crazy?" Gamon asked.

I was about to tell him that only idiots and amateurs jumped to conclusions like that—but I stopped. I didn't expect any kind of intellectual discourse from a high school student running an aggregator blog.

"There were about forty thousand holes on the ceiling..."

"What?! You counted them all?" Gamon's eyes went wide.

It was kind of amazing how he could get surprised at every little thing.

"I would never do something so inefficient as count them all individually. All you need to do is count the number of rows, and the number of holes in a row. It took less than fifteen minutes."

Gamon didn't seem satisfied with my answer. He was still glaring at me.

"Right, right. Sorry. So what was the message hidden in the holes?"

"Just like you said, they were encoded letters."

"CODE! ☆ CODE! ☆ DYING? DINING? KITCHEN! ☆" Narusawa seemed unable to keep up with the conversation, so she was interrupting at irregular intervals. The word "inappropriate" probably didn't exist in this large-breasted woman's dictionary.

I decided to ignore this mysterious creature.

"Well, basically, the whole ceiling was covered in letters."

"Letters on the ceiling?! That's really surprising!" Gamon wanted to look good for Aikawa, so he kept interrupting, too. "Did you hear that, Myu-Pom? It was my idea that they were letters! Even Zonko told me I was smart!"

"Wow, you're amazing, Gamo!"

"Who's Zonko?" I asked. Was he talking about some other girl?

"Right, right. Zonko is this radio." Gamon showed me the bag he had slung over his shoulder. Inside was a very old-looking radio.

"What are you talking about?"

"Oh, this thing talks all the time."

"Gamo, are you talking about that again...?" Aikawa seemed bothered.

Evidently, Gamon was delusional. This wasn't a surprise. I'd had that feeling already. And actually, "talking" was what a radio was supposed to do...

I decided to ignore Gamon's words, just like I was ignoring

Narusawa's. Japanese people had the bad habit of interrupting stories and dragging out meetings.

I tapped my fingers lightly on the photo of the pegboard.

"More specifically, it was using a format called Baudot code."

"Baudot code?"

Everyone looked confused.

"It doesn't surprise me that you haven't heard about it. It was a form of letter encoding used as a storage medium for PCs over 50 years ago."

"A storage medium? You mean like a hard disk?"

"Old computers used a kind of paper tape called punch tape to record data by punching five rows of holes. It was used as a means of read/write storage for computers, but before that, it was used for telegraphs." It had a long history.

Evidently there were also versions that used six or eight rows instead of five, but I'd been able to decode my father's message using the five-row version.

"Hey! Hey! I saw that in an old movie, maybe!" Narusawa had been spacing out with drool oozing down the side of her mouth, but suddenly, she jumped up and began to do little hops. It seemed she was able to form a mental image of punch tape in her head.

"So you punch holes in tape...then the holes on the ceiling were...?!"

"It's the same thing as binary. You can either leave a hole open, or close it. If it's open, it's '0.' If it's closed, it's '1.' And then you just treat it as Baudot code. For example, '00011' is 'A,' and '11001' is 'B.'" I used my right hand to count in binary.

"I see. Or not. I don't get it," Gamon said.

"Well, it doesn't matter. By using this code, five dots can be converted into a single letter."

"Man, that sounds like a pain in the ass. So you need to look at fifty dots just to get ten letters?"

Gamon had actually pointed out something intelligent for once.

"That's right."

"So what was the message on the ceiling?" Aikawa seemed worried as she motioned for me to continue.

"That's right. That's what's important."

"Imp? ☆ Or Tant! ☆"

"Fine. I'll get started. I'll tell you. It was…names."

"A name?" Gamon stood up in shock. "It wasn't 'Ririka Nishizono,' was it?"

"Who's that?"

"Huh? It's not her?"

"It wasn't a single individual's name, actually."

I paused for a moment—and then took a deep breath before speaking very carefully.

"It was the names of 256 people."

I could hear everyone gulp.

Everyone in the room had reached a single conclusion, and fallen silent.

"I took a random section and decoded it, only to get the name 'KAMATA NORIYUKI.'"

"Who's that?"

"No idea. There were others, like 'USUI SACHIKO' and 'SHIRAYAMA TORU.'"

"U-um?!" Aikawa leaned forward, more eager than she'd been a moment ago.

"Was one of the names 'Chizu Kawabata'?"

"Is that someone you know?'

"...Yes. My best friend."

"I'm not sure. It would take a long time to decode all the names."

"I see..." Aikawa's shoulders were slumping.

"Wait, why didn't you decode them all? Even if it takes time, it's still worth doing, right?" Gamon sounded angry.

"The decoding is a simple task. There's no reason for me to do it. Now that I've come up with the interpretation algorithm, anyone can do the rest. Any idiot, I should say. Why don't *you* do it?"

"...Grr..."

"Instead, I chose to spend my time on a series of letters that I found more inexplicable."

"An inexplicable series of letters?"

"Yes. After every one of the 256 names, there was a ten-character series of strange letters. I thought about it all night, and didn't come up with an answer."

"I see..." Gamon suddenly had a nasty grin on his face. "So the famous Sarai's throwing in the towel... LOL!"

"I haven't thrown in the towel. I just haven't had time to finish analyzing the problem."

"Right, right. Whatever you say, man."

Gamon wants to know the answer, right? Why does he keep provoking me? It's not going to help him with anything.

"Um, was there any kind of rule or something for those last ten letters?" Aikawa seemed to have run out of patience with Gamon, and she knocked him out of the way to ask her question.

"The last seven were always the same. 'EEQTUWI.'"

"Umyu? That doesn't sound like it means anything, huh?" chimed in Narusawa.

"But the three in front were always different. The most common was 'QEQ.' Then there was also 'QQQ,' 'POQ,' 'QRQ,' 'QPQ,' 'QEY,' 'QEQ,' 'QQY,' 'QWQ,' and 'PIQ.' There was only one 'QQY' that I saw, for example."

"So there's some kind of rule for them, but you don't know what they mean?" asked Aikawa. "Maybe Toko would know..."

"Toko?"

"She's an editor at *Mumuu.*"

"Huh? Seriously?" Gamon shouted excitedly.

"Seriously."

"Introduce me."

"Oh, sure. That's fine. I'll do that."

"Thanks...um, anyway." Gamon turned back to me and slowly raised his hand. "By the way, those 256 people, they have to be...*them,* right?"

I knew what Gamon was trying to say.

Of course, so did Aikawa and Narusawa.

256.

It was a special number, mathematically. It was also a good number for computers to work with. On old 8-bit computers, the highest number you could show was 256. But in Japan right now, that number had an entirely different meaning. For the past few days, you couldn't look anywhere on the media or the internet without seeing it.

"Maybe this is...a list of the victims who were found in Inokashira Lake."

Everyone fell silent and the air became heavy once more.

"By the way, um, did you try matching it with the publicly available list of victims?" asked Aikawa.

"No. I haven't. I only decoded about ten randomly picked names.

"After that, I used all my brain's memory capacity towards solving the mystery of the other letters. I thought about it all during work today, but I'd gotten nowhere."

The news had still only announced about half of the victims' names, and the internet was buzzing with rumors about secret conspiracies and government censorship. But it was still a mystery why it was taking so long.

Gamon suddenly pointed a finger at Ryotasu.

"Okay, Ryotasu. You decode them."

"Me? Hmm, okay! I didn't understand what Sarai-kyun said at ALL! Not in the slightest! So you can just leave it to me! ♪ "

"Wait—"

"..."

This Narusawa girl seemed to have a few screws loose after all.

She was always so...innocent...no matter what was going on around her... It was hard to understand.

"She's no good. Somebody has to do it. Okay, who should it be, then?" Gamon was refusing to volunteer himself. It was obvious that he'd spent his whole life foisting off the hard jobs onto someone else.

"Do you want me to do it?" Aikawa raised her hand reluctantly.

Gamon's eyes were shining, but surprisingly, Narusawa shook her head.

"Myu, you don't have time for that."

"Huh?"

"You just focus on your friend. Okay?"

"Narusawa..."

Friend? Does she mean Chizu Kawabata?

"But then who's going to do it?"

"Gamon should do it." Since they were taking so long, I chose to decide things myself, but Narusawa interrupted again.

"Gamotan can't do it either. He doesn't have time for that."

"You don't?"

"...Y-yeah. That's right. Yeah. That's exactly right. I'm busy."

Gamon was trying his best to look away from everyone. That meant he was lying. He was easy to understand.

At this rate, we weren't going to get anywhere. *I guess we'll just have to put off the list, then.*

"By the way, you said the name 'Ririka Nishizono.' Who is that?"

"...It's someone I'm thinking might be the real killer, not that I have any evidence."

"The real killer?" *Did he mean the person who'd killed my dad? But he didn't have any evidence, he'd said.* "Who are they?"

"An ero-doujin writer."

"What did you say?"

"The person who drew this," Gamon said, and he took out of his bag—a shady-looking doujin with two men holding each other on the cover.

"Hey, can I go home?"

"W-wait! There's a reason for this!"

▸ site 48: Yuta Gamon

When I showed everybody Ririka Nishizono's *The Bottom of the Dark Water* they all freaked out.

Sarai, especially. It took 30 minutes to stop him from going home.

"Stay away from me, you pervert high-schooler!" he cried.

"Why? Are you calling me a homo? Takes one to know one!"

"How many homo-friends~ ♪ can Gamotan make? ♪"

"I didn't realize you were into that, Gamo... I don't really understand, but every person is different. I won't say that it's wrong. Good luck with it," said Myu-Pom.

"Right, right. Showing half-hearted understanding is the most hypocritical thing you can do! And I've been telling you for a while now, I'm not gay!"

I like *normal* ero-doujin!

"More importantly, listen to me! This ero-doujin isn't a normal ero-doujin!"

"Right. It's a gay doujin, right? You told us that," said Sarai.

"It doesn't *matter* if it's gay! This book foretells Dr. Hashigami's death!"

"What?"

"Huh?"

"Poyah?"

Everyone finally shut up.

Jeez... They didn't need to freak out so much just because they saw a gay doujin...

"What do you mean?"

Sarai looked confused, so I opened up the doujinshi and showed him the inside. I'd opened the book to the middle of the five stories, the third one.

"See that guy lying on the ground with his tooth yanked out?"

"Hold on," said Sarai. "You're not telling me that something like that makes it a 'prophecy,' are you?"

I could see the words "waste of time" written on Sarai's angry face. Since it was his own father we were talking about, maybe that made sense.

"No, no! It's not just that. A small part of the internet's noticed this. But there's one more thing that I saw." I turned the page again. "Look here. At the right hand of the victim, as he lies on the ground. Doesn't it look like his index finger is strangely extended?"

"Depending on how you look at it, maybe..." Myu-Pom was tilting her head, unconvinced.

"If you draw a straight line from where his finger points..." I quickly grabbed a straw off the counter and used it to make a line on the page. "Look at what the man's pointing at. It's some kind of strange object in a frame."

"Cola! ☆ Colon! ☆"

"Ryotasu, look closer."

"Poyaya?"

"What is this...?" Only Sarai seemed to notice what the man was pointing to.

"When you look closer, this doesn't say 'COLA,' it says 'CODE.'"

"..."

"CODE. I told you about it, right Sarai? It was Dr. Hashigami's dying message that I found at the scene."

The only people who could've known this were me, the killer, the mystery man who'd come in after me, and the police. And all of that was after the killing. And the police, for some reason, had hidden the fact from Sarai that his dad left a dying message.

"This doujinshi was published at winter Comiket. You get the rest, right?"

That meant that this book had the same word as the dying message the professor had left.

"Gamo, I'm sorry to interrupt, but don't you think it's just a coincidence?" asked Myu-Pom.

"Huh?"

Sarai nodded at Myu-Pom. "It probably is. CODE is a very common word. And it's more likely the author changed what it said for copyright reasons. This isn't enough evidence on its own. Unless there are a minimum of three commonalities, a coincidence is just a coincidence."

Grr...

There actually was another thing that the book and reality had in common. The man's tooth had been torn out and carried off. But I couldn't tell them that.

My fingers suddenly moved to the gold tooth key in my pocket.

If I told Sarai and the others about this, they'd lose even more faith in me as a person. But I didn't have a choice. Otherwise, they wouldn't believe that Ririka Nishizono was suspicious.

Come on, tell them! Tell them everything! They're the only allies you've got right now...!

"A-anyway," I stuttered, "I think you should take a closer look at it. Y-you might understand a little of what I'm talking about... Maybe. Hahaha."

Oops...

In the end, regardless of what I wanted to do, I didn't say it. I was a little shocked at my own wimpiness... Just trying to bring up the courage to talk about it made my heart beat like a drum.

"I-I'm begging you, guys..."

I couldn't look Sarai in the eye. Sarai sighed and flipped through the doujinshi. I would've preferred he read it carefully, instead of just skimming it.

"Are you trying to tell me this is synchronicity?" he griped. "But that hasn't been explained in the scientific sense. Synchronicity is just the result of assuming several coincidences have meaning. The world is filled with coincidences. Trying to bring meaning to every coincidence is how conspiracy theories got started. It would be better to say that human curiosity and imagination make the world more complicated than it should be. Delusions amplify a person's imagination. That's exactly what's going on with the sexual depictions in this book. They're very different than reality."

God, shut up... I put my hands over my ears in annoyance.

"Are you sure about that?" Master Izumin, who'd been quiet,

interrupted. He'd heard our whole conversation from behind the counter, so it was strange that he hadn't said anything until now. Evidently, he'd finally run out of patience. "Sure you're not just being cynical, Sarai? Conspiracy theories exist. It's more fun to believe that."

I appreciate the support, Master Izumin, but Sarai's not going to believe that...

"I have no intention of denying the existence of every conspiracy theory, but you can't deny that their proponents are constantly making impossible logical leaps in their arguments, can you? And simply ignoring anything that would go against their theory."

Sarai's counterattack shut Master Izumin up completely. It didn't seem like he had anything he could say. There was nothing I could say, either. Maybe I was wrong about Ririka Nishizono being the real killer...

"...Hmm? Wait a second. This is—" Sarai suddenly stopped flipping. His eyes were on a certain page.

...What is it?

"What's wrong?" I asked.

"This...number..."

I peered over at the doujin. He had it open to the last page. Even when I tried to follow the story, the last page had nothing to do with what came before it. It was weird. Instead of the end of the story, there was just a picture of a car.

Had Sarai...found something on this page?

"Do you recognize that car?"

"No, that's not it. It's not the car—"

Sarai's fingers were shaking.

"What is it? Tell me! What did you find?!"

His finger was pointing at—

"The license plate?"

Unlike a Japanese license plate, this one consisted of seven numbers.

"3315728...?"

"What's wrong with the number?" Myu-Pom was looking at the doujin, too.

Sarai, however, had closed his eyes and was mumbling to himself.

"That's right... That's it... You can use Baudot code. So that was it..."

"Come on, Sarai, tell me!"

I grabbed his shoulders and shook him. He opened his eyes and slammed his fist down on the paper in front of him—the picture of the holes in the study ceiling.

"It's 'EEQTUWI.'"

"Huh?"

"It's the 'EEQTUWI' that I couldn't decode! Baudot code can be used for numbers as well as the alphabet! '00001' is the letter E, but if you look at the conversion chart...it's also the number 3."

"You're not saying...?"

"EEQTUWI can be converted to numbers. And those numbers are..." Sarai adjusted his glasses in an attempt to calm down. "3315728. It's the same as this license plate!"

"...!"

The number on the license plate...matched the one in the professor's study!

"Hey, Gamon! Who wrote this book?!" Sarai whacked me in the chest with the doujinshi. "Who is Ririka Nishizono?"

"Sh-she's an ero-doujin author! I've never met her!"

"You're not telling me she really prophesied the future, are you? That's impossible! That's too occult for me to believe. If there's some explanation that doesn't involve the occult, it's—"

"It's that Ririka Nishizono is the killer. Right?"

"..." Sarai's expression was getting sterner. He'd finally realized how dangerous this doujinshi was.

"There's contact info in the afterword Did you try contacting her?"

"No..."

There was an email address written there but I hadn't had the courage to contact her.

"Gamon, I'm sorry for doubting you." Sarai bowed. "Whether or not this is a prophecy, I've taken an interest in Ririka Nishizono. I'll investigate this EEQTUWI matter myself. Was there anything else that you saw?"

"Huh? Um..." I couldn't tell him about the gold tooth key, but—

"Are you hiding something?" he asked.

"Huh? Huh?"

"You've been refusing to look me in the eye. And you keep saying 'Huh?' That's evidence that you understand my questions and are pretending not to. Is there something you're feeling guilty about? Something else you haven't told me? You keep putting your hand in your pocket. What's in there? You just looked away again. If you're hiding something, then knock it off, asshole! I showed you my dad's study. You need to show me everything you're hiding."

"Uh..."

He was so observant! His superpowers felt even more real than Myu-Pom's.

He was glaring at me and I couldn't even move a finger.

It felt like even the smallest twitch would betray to him what I was hiding.

▸ site 49: MMG

"What's going on with the signals of the 'dead' who fell into the spirit world. Are they 'alive'?"

Takasu didn't nod in answer to Manitoba's question, but he didn't shake his head, either.

"The numbers are getting better," he said.

"Once monitoring after death is possible, the plan will move forward immensely. Couldn't we incorporate not just the second generation, but the third generation into our experiment as well?" Yamaha asked.

Manitoba frowned. "Why are there 256 people per cage, anyway? Couldn't you more finely tune that number?"

"Due to issues with the system, that's impossible," Hatoyama said. "The system itself is very old, you see."

Manitoba still looked unsatisfied, but he didn't say anything.

"The disposal of the 256 into Inokashira Lake was unexpected, but as a result, we proved that 'Odd Eye' is ready for practical use. In that sense, the disposal of the first generation, as well as the cage, didn't go to waste." There was a subtle hint of reproach towards Takasu in Hatoyama's words.

But Takasu pretended not to notice, and nodded, satisfied.

"If we can solve the problem of the prison of time, the new World System will finally be complete, and we will acquire the Spirit World." He spread his arms and looked up to the sky in his usual overdramatic fashion.

"And that means we will control this world forever."

▸ site 50: Yuta Gamon

"Well, whatever." Sarai sighed and looked away from me.

How long had passed since I'd fallen silent in answer to his questions? It felt like a long time, but maybe it wasn't even thirty seconds.

It looked like Sarai had thankfully given up on getting any answers out of me. Knowing him, maybe he'd decided it was a waste of time.

"But I think we do need to look closer into what's in this doujinshi."

"I-I agree with that," I muttered meekly.

"May I look at it too?" Myu-Pom, who'd been holding her breath as she watched the two of us talk, took the doujin. She flipped through the pages.

"Um, Myu-Pom, what do you think about BL?" I asked.

"What do you mean?'

"D-does it turn you on?"

"Gamo, that doesn't matter now—" And then she gasped. "Oh, look!" Her eyes went wide as she looked at one of the pages in the doujinshi.

Something was wrong.

"What is it?" Was there another secret hidden in this thing? Was it possible for all the stuff in this book to just line up with reality like that? How many prophecies could you fit in a single volume?

Ririka Nishizono was terrifying...!

"Th-this is..." She was pointing at a page from the second story in the book, where the keyhole of the Kotoribako was.

I shuddered when I saw it.

I'd been thinking about the Kotoribako as well.

It felt like the lock on it matched the gold tooth key. I'd actually put the tip of the gold tooth key up against the page and it had seemed to match. This didn't feel like a coincidence to me, but I still couldn't mention the key.

"Kotoribako? What about it?"

"..." Myu-Pom was going pale.

The second story was this creepy thing about some smug albino jackass who had a box called the Kotoribako to put birds in. In the story, he had a threesome with two "Gods of Fortune." The protagonist was this annoying jerk who always had a grin on his face, and was extremely cynical. And for some reason, these two Gods of Fortune fell in love with him, and they had sex.

The Kotoribako ended up having very little to do with the story.

Which only made its presence even more strange.

It was like the box existed first, and then the author tried to force the BL story to go along with it.

"What's wrong with the Kotoribako?" I asked again, but Myu-Pom had wrapped her hands around herself and started to shake.

"Kotori... Kotoriba... Kotoribako..." She was clearly panicking. I couldn't explain why.

It was kind of like when she'd burst into tears when she saw Sarai's vision during the Niconico Live Fortune-Telling.

"What is a Kotoribako?" Myu-Pom just barely managed to squeak out the words.

"All I know is that it's some kind of dangerous box you can see in a creepypasta online." I'd looked it up myself, but even on 2chan it was treated as a word you weren't supposed to search for. Nobody wanted to talk about it.

Sarai and Master Izumin didn't seem to know anything about it either. Neither did Ryotasu, obviously.

Myu-Pom took her cell phone out and made a call.

"I'll ask Toko..."

Wait, was that the *Mumuu* editor she just mentioned?

"Um, hello! Toko?" Myu-Pom began to ask whoever she was talking to on the phone about the Kotoribako.

Just like you'd expect from an editor at *Mumuu*, she evidently knew about the Kotoribako. Myu-Pom put the phone on speaker so that we could all hear.

"So Toko, what exactly is the Kotoribako?"

The woman on the phone began to speak in a clear, rapid voice.

"Just from the name, you might think it's some kind of birdcage. But it's much more...brutal...than that."

"Brutal...?" Myu-Pom said.

Was it something from a ghost story or something? How did I not know this? As a guy running an occult aggregator, that might not be good—but that thought fled from my mind when I heard her next words.

"The Kotoribako...is a child-taking box."

When I heard her say that, my hair stood up on end.

"...No." Myu-Pom was shocked, too.

Child-taking? Just the name sounded bad.

"What's the story behind it...?"

"It used to be a ghost story from the internet. The rumor is that it got its start in Shimane Prefecture, but there's no real source on it, so it's possible that someone just made it up."

So this is an occult thing, then?

"The Kotoribako is made from lots of different wooden blocks. It's not a normal box. It's a series of complicated parts shaped like a square, and you have to open it in a special order."

"You see things like that sold as gifts, don't you?" Sarai knew about something similar, evidently.

"Yes. They're a traditional craft in Hakone. But the Kotoribako is something totally different. One theory says that it was made around the 1860s. It's supposed to be about twenty cubic centimeters, I think."

The one in Ririka Nishizono's manga had been about that size.

"That's a lot bigger than the ones in Hakone."

"Yes. This is a ritual item. It's intended to curse people, and kill them. The box has an effect on the area around where it's laid. Anyone affected by the curse has all their organs ripped apart and they die as they cough up their own blood. And the curse's effects are limited to women and children."

"A curse... Do you mean like black magic?!" I asked.

The name Aria Kurenaino came to mind.

"No. This is a Japanese story. Western magic has nothing to do with it."

"Y-you're right..."

"Supposedly it was originally made by villagers who were suffering under the local ruler's heavy taxes. You can bury it in the garden of the person you want to curse, and all their family's women and children will die, until their family finally ceases to exist. That's why it's the 'child-taking' box."

That sounded like a very powerful ritual item... It was probably a rare item with an S-Rank curse status. Like if you used it, the target would die...and so would you.

"The issue is how it's made. It's brutal."

All of us were totally focused on Toko's story now. Even Ryotasu, who never focused on anything, was biting her lip and listening. For my part, my hands were soaking with sweat. I pressed them against my pants to wipe it off.

"First, you fill the box with the blood of a female animal. Supposedly a fox or chicken was often used."

A female animal...

"Then you would let it sit for a week, and then add a part from the body of a child who'd undergone mabiki."

Huh?

"At the time, it was normal for people to do what they called 'mabiki,' or culling, where they'd kill unneeded children. You'd put a part of that child's body inside the box. What part it was depended on the age of the child. If it was a newborn baby, it was the umbilical cord, or the tip of the index finger. And their blood, drawn while they were alive. For a child younger than seven, it was their blood and the tip of their index finger. For a child younger than ten, just the first part of the index finger. Once that's done, you seal the box and send it to the person you want to curse."

"That really is brutal..." I was starting to feel sick.

"Gamon, you run an occult aggregator blog, don't you? Aren't you used to scary stories by now?" Sarai smirked.

"I-I'm not scared..."

Shut up, Sarai! Stop coolly analyzing my facial expression! Honestly, I felt like I was about to throw up.

"The effects of the curse change depending on the number of sacrificed children."

"Huh? It's not just one child?"

"What you call the box changes depending on the number of sacrifices. One, and you call it an ippo. Two, a niho. Three, a sanpo. Four, and it's a shippo. Five, a goho. Six, and it's a roppo. Seven, a chippo. Eight, and it's a hakkai. More than eight, and the box becomes too strong, and it's dangerous. In some cases, its effects can last more than a hundred years."

Eight kids...

So, there was enough hate put into that box that whoever made it would be willing to kill eight children...

Just imagining it made me shiver.

"By the way, I really shouldn't be telling you this, but I learned this from a source connected to *Mumuu...*" Toko lowered her voice.

"One of the Kotoribako is somewhere in Kichijoji."

"What...?!" I cried.

Kichijoji's got way *too many curses.*

"Listen, you guys. The Kotoribako is a really nasty thing. Don't think about looking for it. Got it?"

"Thanks, Toko."

"Huh? Wait, Miyuu?!"

Myu-Pom said thanks and hung up the phone.

I wish I could've talked to the editor at Mumuu *some more...*

"Wahhh... I'm not gonna be able to go to the bathroom tonight..." Ryotasu was crying. I thought she was unusually quiet. The crying must have been why.

Just like Toko said, the Kotoribako was too dangerous. I was too scared to want to get close to it. Even if I did find a real one, I wouldn't want to touch it.

But maybe the Kotoribako had something to do with Dr. Hashigami's murder. Since it was in Ririka Nishizono's doujinshi, I couldn't say that it didn't.

"So, Myu-Pom, what's up with the Kotoribako? It looks like it's bothering you somehow."

Myu-Pom had been acting weird ever since she'd seen it in the doujinshi. She looked scared and exhausted.

"If... If I can, I want to try and find that Kotoribako right now..."

"You want to search for it? Are you crazy?"

And then Myu-Pom told me that her friend had been missing for a week, and that the last thing she'd said had been "Birdie Bo."

She flipped through the pages.

Was that a coincidence, or was that part of Ririka Nishizono's prophecy?

And did the Kotoribako have something to do with Dr. Hashigami's death?

"It's going to be hard to find it without knowing more than that it's in Kichijoji." Sarai frowned.

"Think we might find something online?" I booted up my laptop and ran a search for "Kichijoji Kotoribako."

But I didn't find anything.

I tried a bunch of other methods, but none of them felt like they were going to work.

So, we were stuck then…

"Um, Gamo, you said that this doujinshi predicts the future, right?" asked Myu-Pom.

"Hmm? Y-yeah."

"Then are there maybe hints in it?"

"Hints, huh…"

The Kotoribako story was about a man with a box having a threesome with two (male) Gods of Fortune.

If there were a hint in here, what would it be?

It might look like just a BL book, but it definitely had more information in it than you'd think. So there must be some kind of meaning to the two "Gods of Fortune."

"This is the only story with a shrine…" Sarai pointed out.

He was right. The only people the main character slept with were the Gods of Fortune, and most of it was set at a shrine, with several panels dedicated to describing it.

"In other words, the Kotoribako is at a shrine?" That felt a little too obvious to me, but it made sense. If it was that powerful, the safest thing to do would be to seal it away somewhere holy.

I decided to run a search for how many shrines there were in Kichijoji.

"There are three shrines in Kichijoji according to this map. Tamamitsu Shrine, Musashino Hachimangu Shrine, and Yaeda Shrine. If you extend the area to Mitaka and Nishi-Ogikubo, there's more."

"Wasn't there a shrine in Inokashira Park?"

Myu-Pom nodded in response to Sarai's question. "Benten Shrine, right? I've been there."

If the shrine in Ririka Nishizono's doujinshi was based off one in Kichijoji, we might be able to find something in common.

"Can we pin it down?" I asked.

"Ririka Nishizono isn't that great an artist." Sarai sighed.

"And it doesn't look like she traced from a picture either. The perspective is all messed up. It looks like she's just drawing haphazardly," he continued.

That would make ID'ing it hard.

"If the torii arch were in it, we might be able to narrow it down a little."

"The torii?"

"There are different kinds of torii arches at shrines. I think there are about sixty variations."

Huh? Seriously? I had no idea.

Way to go, Sarai-kyun. You're like a walking encyclopedia.

"But...there's no torii arch in this doujinshi."

He was right. There were no torii arches drawn. The only scenes with the Gods of Fortune were drawn inside the shrine grounds.

"The shrine's supposed to be pretty big, so wouldn't it be something like Musashino Hachimangu?" I asked. I checked with street view, and of the three shrines in Kichijoji, Yaeda Shrine was tiny. It was basically just an arch and a shrine building. We could eliminate that one, maybe.

That is, if Ririka Nishizono was being careful with what she drew.

There was a chance that her shrine had nothing to do with a real one. If that were the case, then we were wasting our time here.

"Are these two Gods of Fortune from the seven Gods of Fortune? If so, then doesn't that mean it's probably Benten Shrine? He's one of them." Myu-Pom's idea was a good one, but...

"These two are supposed to be Gods of Fortune," I said, "but they don't actually do anything blessing-y."

Each of the seven Gods of Fortune was famous and distinct, so if you were drawing one of them, you'd add in parts of their costume or something to make them recognizable.

Ririka Nishizono's gods weren't anything more than normal, handsome men.

Of course, that wasn't a problem. This was an original doujinshi. She could draw whatever she wanted.

But there was no way to tell if one of the gods, or perhaps both, were supposed to be Benzaiten. We were never told their names, for one thing.

I thought about going to the park to check, but Inokashira Park was closed right now.

"Wait, wasn't that place a temple, not a shrine?" Myu-Pom asked.

"Oh, was it?"

"I don't think...there was an arch."

"Which means..." I used my laptop to search the area around Kichijoji again. "Maybe we were mistaken to limit ourselves to shrines."

There were about six temples around Kichijoji. But that didn't mean we'd found any kind of new clue. Instead of having three places to search, we now had nine.

"..."

I realized that everyone had fallen silent.

The debate had reached an end.

This single doujinshi wasn't going to give us any critical hints.

"I'm going to the bathroom." I headed for the bathroom to clear my head.

The bathroom was dark and moody, like always. There were all kinds of flyers and things pasted up on the walls, and I always felt a little uneasy in there.

As I relieved myself, I looked at the flyers, until my eyes happened to stop on a small poster the size of an ordinary piece of paper.

"Make a Pilgrimage to the Seven Gods of Fortune in Kichijoji, Musashino"

"What a coincidence." We'd been talking about the seven Gods of Fortune, and here I was staring at a poster for an event involving them.

What a coincidence. Or was it a coincidence? Maybe there was a hint here.

"Hmm?"

It was a bus tour that was held every January. The tour visited shrines and temples relating to the seven Gods of Fortune in Kichijoji.

The one in Inokashira was included in the tour as well. There was also Anyoji, Musashino Hachimangingu, and Daihozenji.

Enmeiji and Kizuki Taisha were pretty far apart. Kizuki Taisha was two stations down at Musashisakai Station, and Enmeiji was in a hard-to-get-to place near Musashino University.

That explained why there was a bus tour. It would be really hard to visit all six spots on your own.

"Hmm? Six? Even though there's seven gods?" *Did I count wrong?*

After I finished and flushed, I leaned forward to take a closer look at the pamphlet.

I followed the stops on the tour in order.

"Inokashira Benzaiten. Musashino Hachimangu, Anyoji, Daihozenji, Enmeiji, Kizuki Taisha... Huh? There really are only six."

Why was there one missing?

I looked even closer, and quickly found the answer.

Each temple, or shrine, had one god in it. Musashino Hachimangu was where Daikokuten was, and Ebisu could be found at Kizuki Taisha. But Enmeiji was a coincidence. There were two Gods of Fortune there: Bishamonten and Juroten...

"Is this..." All the hair on my body stood on end. "Two Gods of Fortune?!"

Wait...was that it? I ripped down the poster and ran from the bathroom.

"Guys! Look! Look at this!" I showed them all the poster.

A wave of surprise went through them as I told them about the two Gods of Fortune at Enmeiji.

"It makes sense...but is this the answer...?" asked Sarai.

"The Kotoribako is at Enmeiji...?" Myu-Pom asked.

"It's worth going, isn't it?" I asked.

"But, but!" Ryotasu looked a little scared. "Isn't it dangerous? The Kotoribako is bad, right?"

"If we just go look, it should be fine—"

And then I heard the quiet, but clear, voice of a woman. "Oh my. How brave."

I turned towards the voice in shock.

At some point, an astonishingly beautiful girl in a long black coat, with long, lush hair, had opened the door and come into the café.

It was a sudden visitor. Of course, we hadn't reserved Blue Moon or anything, so it wasn't strange for anybody else to show up.

This girl had an aura about her that made her hard to approach, and she gave each of us an ice-cold glance.

As all of us stood there in shock, Ryotasu spun around and pointed to the girl.

"It's the witch! ☆"

The witch...?

"Aria Kurenaino..." Myu-Pom whispered. It was only then that I realized who she was.

Wait, Aria Kurenaino?!

"U-uwah! She's come to curse us!" I hid behind Ryotasu's back, quickly. "I knew it! I found the truth hidden in Ririka Nishizono's doujinshi, and her coconspirator Aria Kurenaino has come to kill me with her curse! It's so obvious now! Sarai, she's a black-magic agent! Her job is to kill people with curses!"

"Calm down, Gamon!" Sarai yelled at me, annoyed. "There's no such things as curses!"

"But—"

"I don't know who Ririka Nishizono is, but..." Aria whispered calmly.

Of course, I had no way of knowing if that was true or not.

"I'm very interested in what I just heard you say."

"What you heard us say? But when? You just got here."

"More precisely, it was relayed to me. It was my partner who heard the story—" And then Aria licked her lips a little, and narrowed her eyes.

"A devil."

I shivered.

I imagined that when she said that, the temperature in the room dropped a little.

Everyone took a step back from her, as if they were feeling an invisible pressure.

Was she...serious? Did she have a real devil serving her? And this devil had heard everything we'd said? Between her words and the fact that she was dressed in all black, I normally would've written her off as some delusional goth girl.

But not now.

The way she moved and acted made it seem like everything she was saying was real.

It felt like she was telling the truth. It was like her magic had put a charm spell on me. Or maybe her voice just had the power to brainwash?

Aria looked at each of us slowly: me, Sarai, then Ryotasu, and then Myu-Pom.

"*Hmph*. How stupid." Sarai was the first to speak. "Black magic? And a devil? So, you're bringing your dark fantasy crap into real life, and trying to make a living on it? Disgusting. And now you're telling me you got a message from your devil? Listen, you're still young. Try to limit your jokes to that cosplay fashion sense of yours."

"..." Aria was looking down, silently.

Sarai... That's just what I'd expect of you. You're so strong. But if you get cursed...don't blame me.

"Listen, if you can speak with a devil," he continued, "call him here, would you? I'd love to see him, and to ask him some questions about Greek mythology—"

BANG! CRASH!

"Hyahh!"

"Kyah!"

Sarai suddenly fell silent, and all of us screamed, as something burst—

It was the light bulbs inside the cafe. Two light bulbs...had exploded! What was going on...?

"Th-that's not a bad magic trick. I've seen that done on TV, but still, it's impressive that you can do it with no preparation—" Sarai was trying his best to hang in there.

"Shhh." Aria softly moved her index finger to her lips.

Silence returned to the room. The only sound was the soft crackling of electricity.

When Sarai took a small step back, Aria glanced upwards at the ceiling and smiled a little, and then began to whisper.

This devil...was seriously a devil.

And then she snorted, upset, and turned to me.

"Perhaps this is your punishment for trying to test black magic... No, to test me."

My punishment?! For trying to test her?! Was she talking about how I'd had the girls pretend to want to get back at me for cheating?! I knew it! She was going to kill me! She was going to make my head explode! Like those light bulbs!

"More importantly, shouldn't you hurry?"

"Huh?"

Aria closed her eyes, and acted like she was listening to something.

And this is what she said.

"This world is filled with evil will. And all that evil will is connected

to one great will—"

"Huh...?" *Will? What will? Whose will?*

"It seems that 'we' were mistaken."

"What are you talking about? Who are you talking to?"

"It is a pure being that knows no pain, and one more cruel and merciless than even the will of a devil. The one who holds that large box is..."

"Box... Do you mean Chi...?! I *know* you do! I'm going!" Myu-Pom ran out of the café.

What was she talking about? What was going on?

"What are you planning?!"

She sighed a little, still with a cold look on her face. "It is a young boy...at Enmeiji...who holds the box—" She glanced at Ririka Nishizono's doujinshi, which was sitting on the table.

And told me.

"A young boy whose hair and everything else is pure white."

"What?!"

She meant "the albino jerk"! Just like in the doujinshi! He was the true killer! He was the one who killed Dr. Hashigami! And he was the one who set me up!

I had to hurry. I didn't even have time to worry that this might be a trap set by Aria.

I was overcome by the impulse to capture that white-haired boy as soon as I could.

PARANORMAL SCIENCE NVL
Occultic;Nine
オカルティック・ナイン
THERE IS NO SUCH THING AS THE "OCCULT." IT CAN ALL BE DISPROVED BY SCIENCE.
ONLY THOSE WHO HAVE ACCEPTED EVERYTHING
HAVE THE RIGHT TO KNOW THE TRUTH.

▸ site 51: Miyuu Aikawa

I heard a hollow sound, echoing. *Clack... Clack.*

Master Izumin had called me a taxi to Enmeiji. When I got there, I ran to the main shrine as fast as I could, hoping I'd see Chi.

And then I heard the sound.

It wasn't a loud sound, but the temple was so quiet that it was a little scary, and the sound echoed in my ears.

"What is this sound...?" Gamo had gotten in the taxi with me. He sounded scared.

Supposedly, this was where the young boy with the box was. That's what Gamo had told me in the taxi.

I was disappointed to find out that it wasn't Chi, but maybe the boy might know something.

I just wanted to hear what he had to say as soon as I could—

I didn't want to think about anything else—

I didn't want to *imagine* anything else—

I looked around.

It was probably because the sun had set, but I couldn't see anybody around.

But...I could still hear the sound.

And it wasn't coming at regular intervals.

There was no order to the rhythm. Sometimes the interval would be shorter, and sometimes longer.

"Think it's from over there?" Narusawa—who'd also come with us—pointed to the back of the temple.

As I walked, I could see the main shrine.

And there they were.

Someone was curled up on the ground beneath the eyes of the statue of Bishamonten that was right next to the shrine.

They should have been able to see us coming, but they didn't turn to look at us at all.

They were laughing. It was a tiny laugh, like a snort.

In their hands was something square that looked like a box.

Clack. Clack.

The sound was coming from the box.

"Who are you?" I turned on the flashlight function on my phone.

And in the light, I saw...

"A white...person?"

Close-cropped white hair, skin like snow, and a body and face that was pure white, like it had been dusted with white powder.

"H-he's really here..." Gamo gulped. Even I could tell he was afraid.

I took a step towards the boy.

And then I felt an awful stench in my nostrils.

What was it? I felt sick.

"Myu-Pom, wait. Something's not right about him." Gamo grabbed my shoulder and stopped me.

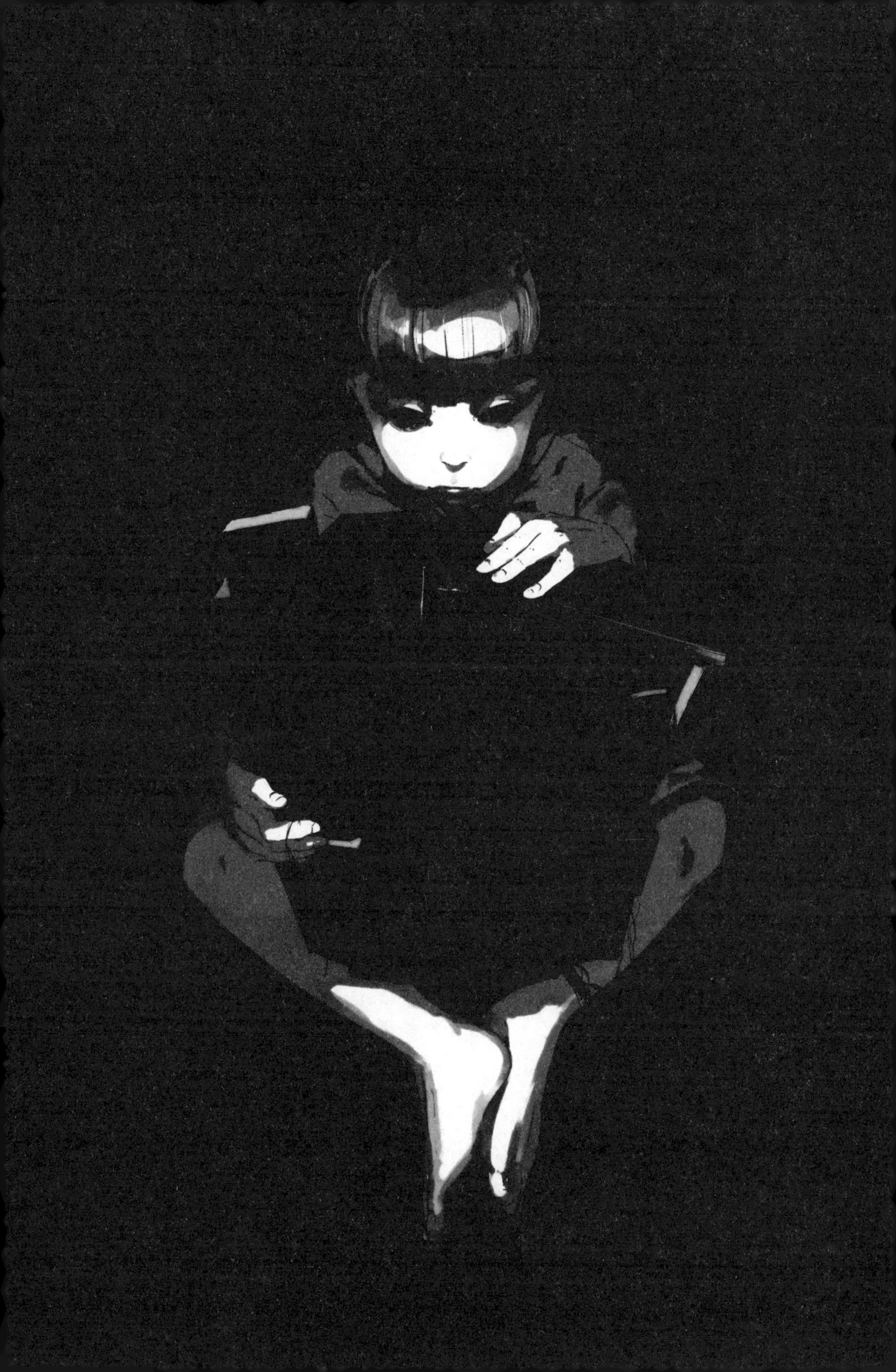

I heard a voice again.

It was like someone talking to themselves, and so quiet it was hard to hear.

The white-haired boy was chortling and whispering something.

"What's wrong? That's weird. This thing must be broken. It won't shut. Hehe." *Clack...*

I heard the sound again.

What was this sound?

"Hey, hey, miss."

"...?!"

Suddenly, he'd spoken to me—at least, it felt that way. Did he call out to me? It was so sudden, I was too shocked to react.

He still wasn't looking at us.

Clack...

The sound, again.

"Looks like I screwed up making the box."

"The...box?" Did he mean the Kotoribako?

"There's, like, manuals and stuff online, but I didn't really look at them. Oh well. But you don't usually look at those, right? Only really serious people do. I'm sure eighty percent of Japanese people don't look at the manual before they start putting something together."

What was he talking about?

Clack...

And what was that hollow sound? I didn't know. I was starting to panic, and I had to know what it was...

My cell phone flashlight shone on the young boy's hands.

Was that... a box? It was about forty cubic centimeters in size.

The surface was really uneven. It wasn't quite square.

It didn't even really *look* like a box. It was more like he'd just piled some blocks together. And around the box were scattered lots of cards. They were trading cards. Just like the card I'd seen in the last photo Chi sent...

"Wh-where's the keyhole?" Gamo was looking hard at the box.

"There isn't one..."

I finally figured out what the sound was.

The box wouldn't hold its shape unless he was pressing on it. Especially the outside. There was a long, vertical block that hadn't been put in very well. If he took his hand off, it couldn't support itself, and popped out.

It was the sound of him pushing it back in.

Each time a block flew out, he'd been popping it back in with annoyance.

"I smell blood." This smell... It was blood.

Where was it coming from? Was it the blocks? And then I realized...

The surfaces of the blocks were wet for some reason.

I could see what looked like hair, poking out from in between the gaps in the blocks.

"Hey..." I couldn't take it anymore, so I spoke to the kid.

It wasn't really because of the cold that my voice was shaking...

"Do you know where my friend is? Her name's Chi. Her real name is Chizu Kawabata. She's a first-year student at Seimei High..."

"I need a sacrifice!" The boy suddenly looked up.

"Hyah!" I almost fell backwards in surprise but Narusawa caught me.

The young boy grinned and looked back at the box. "A sacrifice needs to go inside the Kotoribako. And that sacrifice needs to be someone everybody loves, it said on the net. Oh, but I'm a minor, so it's not a crime. Because I'm a minor, you know."

Clack.

Another block got pushed out.

When he moved it back, his hands were slick, too.

"They told me about somebody who could be a good sacrifice. And it's actually this super-popular high school girl that Moritsuka was telling me about a while ago. I figured she'd be the perfect sacrifice, but..." He took his hand off the box, and another block pocked out.

He'd been doing that again and again. It felt like something I shouldn't be looking at.

I wanted to run away, *now*.

But I couldn't take my eyes off his hands.

"Why?" I asked, without even realizing I'd done so. "Why is your hand wet? Why is it red?"

But he ignored me.

"But, I guess I screwed up."

"Huh?" *He screwed up? What—*

"The sacrifice. Even if I screw up, I'm a minor, so it's not a crime."

"Tell me!" I yelled. "What's...in that box...?" I couldn't even speak anymore.

No more...

"What's wrong? I'm a minor, so it's not a crime." The young boy slowly stood up.

The blocks fell apart again, but he didn't try to fix them.

"I-I'll call the police!!" Gamo said, but the boy just grinned and shrugged.

"The police? Why? I keep telling you. I'm a minor, so I won't get in trouble."

"Answer my question!" That was as loud as I could scream.

"If you want to know, I'll give you this box. It's a failure, but it's halfway made." And then the boy looked at me again.

He had a huge smile on his face. Different than the grin before.

"Myu—"

—How did he know my name?

"—that was you, wasn't it?"

And then the white boy went away, leaving behind the falling-apart box.

"W-wait!" Gamo tried to stop him, but the strange atmosphere around the boy seemed to keep him frozen in place.

The boy vanished, slowly, towards the graveyard behind the temple.

All that was left was the three of us, and the box placed in front of the statue of Bishamonten.

I didn't want to imagine it. I didn't want to see it.

If I saw it, I knew I'd regret it.

Maybe I could use my fortune-telling in my mind on the box's contents. Maybe I could see a vision.

But I was too scared of what I'd see to do it.

No, it was better not to do it.

Don't look inside that box.

I knew not to. I knew not to, but...

I took a step, and then another.

I walked towards the box.

Hey...

What did that boy put in the box? What did he mean by "sacrifice"? What did he mean, he "got it wrong"? How'd he know my name? Why would he give it to me? What is inside this wet, twisted thing that's not even really a box?

I kneeled in front of it, and touched it with my fingertip.

It felt slick.

It was sticky. It was super cold, and I almost jerked my hand away.

It was made of wood, but I imagined it was made of stainless steel. The box was made of wood blocks, piled into a rectangle. And they were all piled together, randomly.

The smell had gotten stronger. It was clearly coming from inside the box.

I could hear something rattling.

A moment later, I realized it was my teeth.

"Myu-Pom!" Gamo yelled to me from behind. "Don't open it!"

I ignored his warning.

I took off the top block.

The smell got worse.

But I didn't care. I kept removing blocks.

I could tell there was less room inside than I thought. The box was pretty big, but there wasn't a lot of room to put anything in it.

"Stop it! Myu-Pom!"

I shook off Gamo's hand.

And I kept tearing down the box.

A piece of hair stuck out of it and wrapped around my finger. It looked like human hair, but I told myself it *couldn't* be. It was just a strange piece of fabric.

The wetness on my hands was cold, and I was losing the feeling in my fingertips. But I still couldn't stop.

This isn't true.

It can't *be true.*

What's inside is something that doesn't matter at all.

It's not a sacrifice. It can't be. I mean, it's the 21st century. This is Japan. It's not a super-long time ago in the past, like the time of the samurai. And this isn't a manga or an anime.

So, my premonition would be wrong. It had to be. *Please be wrong.*

As I prayed...I dismantled half of the box.

And then I saw something shine within it.

I took a deep breath, and looked inside.

I could see a hairpiece with a cute little dog mascot. It was stained red and black.

"Aah...ahh...." I knew it.

It was...

It was the one I wore on my head. I'd given another one to Chi on her birthday, so we could match.

"No..." I reached out my hand for the hairpiece.

But it was dark. I judged the distance wrong.

And I touched the thing that was under it.

It was thick, like yogurt, and it was so disgusting, I quickly yanked back my hand.

"Myu-Pom?! That's enough! Stop it!" Gamo's cell phone flashlight illuminated my hands.

My fingers were covered in pink yogurt mixed with red.

No, that wasn't it. That wasn't yogurt. Despite all that was going on, my brain knew exactly what was happening. This was...

It *had* to be...

This was what was left of Chi's brain.

"NOOOOOOOOOOO!" And then...I passed out.

▸ site 52: Yuta Gamon

Several days had passed since the incident at Enmeiji. After what had happened, Myu-Pom had passed out from the shock and had to be hospitalized. I didn't hear any details about the albino boy, or what was in his box. The papers didn't really report it. But whatever was inside it *was* once human. I knew that.

I hadn't been to Blue Moon once since then. I hadn't been to school, either. I'd stayed in my house the whole time. I'd taken the photo of the ceiling of Dr. Hashigami's study, stretched a copy out on a printer, and kept decoding the list. It took a long time—and was *really* boring—to decode the whole thing myself, but when I finished, I might have access to information even the police didn't.

This was all I had left. This was all I could do.

Just like I thought, the names of the people matched the list of the ones in the 256 Incident. Forty-three names had matched so far. One of them was Yuna Miyamae, the girl who'd been taken to the hospital after playing Kokkuri-san.

Only about 150 of the victims from the 256 Incident had had their names released. So only a few names had matched so far. But if I kept going, eventually all the names should match.

I wasn't sure if I should tell the police. It felt like they were acting weird. I couldn't trust them.

I had my TV on all the time in the living room. A news program was giving an update on the 256 Incident.

"—The police just released a new list of victims. This brings the total number to two hundred, but the remaining fifty-six have yet to be identified."

Oh, perfect timing. If there were new names released, I needed to match them with my list.

"Hey." I heard a voice from the Skysensor. "How long are you going to keep doing that busywork? Shouldn't you leave it to someone else? It's a job for *idiots,* right?" Zonko had been saying that ever since I started. She was getting really annoying.

But whenever Mom came home, Zonko fell silent immediately. It seemed like she was only going to talk when it was just me and her.

"Forget that list," she continued. "Worry about the key. That's more important, right?"

"No, the key's important, but I walked all over and didn't find anything it matched. I don't have a choice."

The Kotoribako that albino boy had didn't have a keyhole. All my memories of that day were like a nightmare.

I still hadn't contacted Ririka Nishizono.

I just wanted to be done going through the list.

When I did, I'd find something. Something that wasn't a nightmare.

I knew there was no point in doing this simple busywork. Zonko had told me I was just trying to escape reality, and she was right. Just the fact that several of the names had matched was enough to justify turning it over to the police. But once I'd started, I felt like I had to continue.

There was *something* in this list.

If Dr. Hashigami had a list of the victims of the 256 Incident a year ago, then there must be something incredible that they all had in common. Maybe he was killed to hide that. Following that logic, I'd cease being a suspect.

"Whew." I decoded another name.

It was a lot more of a hassle than you'd think to decode a name from dots. This was number seventy, finally.

Umm...

"GAMON YUTA—???"

"Here are the names of the newest victims. Tadashi Iguchi. Yoko Ishizuka. Mitsuko Edo. Toyohiko Oba. Yasumi Ogata. Shingo Kaga. Yuta Gamon—"

"Yuta Gamon—"

"Buh?" For some reason, I made a weird noise as the announcer called my name.

"Hey, Zonko! Did you hear that? I'm... I'm a victim, it says! Ahahahaha! That's hilarious, huh? Both the code on the ceiling and the TV news called my name at the same time! Hahaha! What's going on here—"

"Sigh..." Zonko cut me off.

And in a resigned, disappointed voice, she said—

"You found it, huh?"

—BzzzBBzzt—bzzbzzzzt—

PARANORMAL SCIENCE NVL
Occultic;Nine
オカルティック・ナイン
THERE IS NO SUCH THING AS THE "OCCULT." IT CAN ALL BE DISPROVED BY SCIENCE.
ONLY THOSE WHO HAVE ACCEPTED EVERYTHING
HAVE THE RIGHT TO KNOW THE TRUTH.

≫ IMPLANT

A method of treatment that involves cutting open the gums and implanting a false root, then putting a false tooth on top of it. While it can't be removed, unlike typical false teeth it doesn't come loose and you can chew with it like you would a regular tooth.

≫ DOUJIN MANGA

Also called doujinshi. A magazine funded and produced by an individual or small group. Unlike normal magazines, these are not sold through normal distribution channels and are primarily "passed out" at doujin events. (They are never "sold.") Originally, they took the form of literary magazines, but as printing technology improved and the number of manga and anime fans increased, more and more of them took the form of manga. There are many genres of doujinshi, such as original works, derived works, all-ages works, adult works, works for men, and works for women. They are also called "thin books."

≫ SCRAMBLE COMMUNICATIONS

A method of encryption used by places like paid satellite channels and cable TV. The data is encrypted by a simple method of scrambling it to stop people who have not bought the service from watching it. Paid customers are given a decoder that allows them to decrypt the scrambled data and view the channel.

» DODO BIRD

A flightless bird that went extinct in the 1600s in what is now the Republic of Mauritius. The word dodo is Portuguese for "fool." A dodo bird, named "The Dodo," appears in Lewis Carroll's Alice in Wonderland.

» INOKASHIRA PARK

Officially named "Inokashira Onshi Park." A 380,000m² park owned by the city and located in Tokyo between Musashino and Mitaka. Opened in 1917, the park contains Inokashira Lake, as well as the Benzaiten and Inari Shrines, and a zoo called the Natural Culture Park. There is also a stadium grounds in the west park, and in the southeast of the west park, there is a smaller park as well.

» NIKOLA TESLA, WARDENCLYFFE TOWER

An electrical engineer and inventor born in the Austrian Empire (now Croatia). 1856–1943. During his student days, he discovered the fundamental principles behind AC (Alternating Current) electricity. Afterward, he went to America and worked for Edison's company, but he fought with Edison over the differences between AC and DC (Direct Current) power transmission and left the company after only a year. In 1888, he invented the AC power generator and AC motor. In addition, in the 21st century, Tesla's AC power is the primary mode of power transmission. He invented several other things as well, but in 1901, he built the 57-meter-tall "Wardenclyffe Tower" on Long Island, America, as part of his experiments with a wireless power transmission system (The World System). But the experiments never succeeded, and due to both

WWI and a lack of funds, it was torn down. The international unit of measurement for the strength of a magnetic field is a "Tesla."

≫ CNN

Cable News Network. The world's first 24-hour news network. Founded in America in 1980.

≫ REUTERS

A communications company founded in 1851 by Paul Julius Freiherr von Reuter. It's currently owned by the Canadian Thompson Corporation and is known as Thompson Reuters.

≫ 2CHANNEL

The most frequently accessed anonymous message board in Japan. Its catchphrase is "From Hacking to Tonight's Side Dishes," and it covers a huge variety of topics, from standard to underground.

≫ DREDGING

The act of bringing up water from a lake and taking the mud, etc. out to improve water quality. Originally used to maintain the water quality in holding lakes for fields, this has been a part of Japanese culture for centuries.

≫ PEOPLE'S TEMPLE

An American religious organization founded in 1955. At first, it called for the abolition of all forms of discrimination, but its founder, Jim Jones, was overcome by fear of persecution, and it gradually became a cult. In 1978, Jones and over 900 of his followers committed suicide in Guyana, South America.

≫ HARMONICA ALLEY

A shopping and dining area in the backstreets near Kichijoji Station. It has over 100 stores.

≫ TWITTER

A social network that started in 2006 in America. This "mini-blogging" platform allows for posts of up to 140 characters in length. In 2014, it had over 2.4 billion active users worldwide.

≫ 256 INCIDENT

A mass death incident that occurred in the book at Inokashira Park. Yuta Gamon came up with this name because 256 corpses were found.

≫ TORA NO ANA

A manga doujinshi shop. There are over 20 of them all across Japan. In Tokyo, they're concentrated in Akihabara, Shinjuku, and Ikebukuro.

≫ J-CAST

A Japanese news company that was founded in 1997. Over 11 million visitors come to J-CAST sites each month.

≫ BAUDOT CODE

A letter code used for teletype communications. Invented in 1905. In 1931, it was chosen as the standard code for the international

Telex network. In the 21st century, it is no longer used in most cases thanks to the internet.

≫ PUNCH TAPE

Here used to refer to paper or plastic tape used as a memory storage device for computers and electronic calculators. Very commonly used between 1950 and 1970. Data is saved by punching holes in long, thin tape, with the presence or lack of a hole being used to denote the data. Originally there were five rows, but later, this increased to six, seven, or even eight rows.

≫ SYNCHRONICITY

A theory propounded by Swiss analytical psychologist Carl Jung. A meaningful coincidence, like a sudden premonition. When two phenomena possess a similarity or connection in meaning or image, they stick out from the order of time and space. This sticking out is the definition of synchronicity.

PARANORMAL SCIENCE NVL
Occultic;Nine
オカルティック・ナイン
THERE IS NO SUCH THING AS THE "OCCULT." IT CAN ALL BE DISPROVED BY SCIENCE.
ONLY THOSE WHO HAVE ACCEPTED EVERYTHING
HAVE THE RIGHT TO KNOW THE TRUTH.

Afterword

OVERLAP novel readers, my beloved maniacs who are fans of Chiyomaru Studio, members of the Committee of 300, lovers of urban legends, people who believe in the occult, people who don't, people who are cursed, people who can see things that aren't really there, and ghosts who are actually already dead—thank you for reading! Just before I wrote this afterword, I took a shower while imagining occult things. Afterwards, I thought I heard a noise from the hallway, but it turned out to be nothing.

Many lives were lost in the second volume of this book.

But what is "death"? The reason everyone thinks about this is that the death rate is 100%. It's a truth that's coming someday, and you can't avoid it.

There's differing opinions about the afterlife, but there are two types of people in general: those who believe that after death, there's nothing, and those who believe that a world awaits after death.

So now it's time for a personality analysis!

If you chose the former, you're a self-proclaimed scientific believer with a strong heart, like Sarai and Gamota. When you see people who claim to be able to see ghosts, you say to yourself, "They just want attention." But you actually fear death more than those in the second group, and you have a tendency to fear dying alone more than they do.

Also, this type tends to lack in communication skills, and not have many friends. For some reason, you don't believe in ghosts, but you'll happily tell everyone about your belief in aliens. In addition, you don't like taking the long route, and your favorite season is winter.

If you chose the latter, you're more like Myu-Pom and Toko—people who hate being alone. You always try to look on the bright side of things, and if you find someone else who feels the same way, you can become friends quickly. You're interested in many things, and you try your best to help your friends with their problems. You do your best to help others, but your room is always filthy, and you always tell yourself you'll clean it tomorrow. People in this type are easily deceived by shady cults and brainwashed.

Your hobby is traveling. You like variety programs. Your favorite season is summer.

How did I do? Anyway, back to the story.

In the last scene, the hero was confronted with an amazing truth.

Since it's the afterword, I can write without worrying about story spoilers. So, in the second volume, the hero dies (lol). In that scene, Gamota finds his own name on the encoded list of victims from Dr. Hashigami's ceiling, and at the same time hears his name called on the TV.

If that ever happened in real life, it'd be shocking, huh? If it happened to you, could you accept that you were dead? Your body still feels fine, if you pinch your cheek it hurts, and you get hungry, etc.

I wouldn't believe it. "No, wait. This has to be some kind of mistake, lol." And then I'd try to find all kinds of proof that I was alive. If I looked over on the family altar and saw my own photo next to the picture of my dad, I'd think somebody was playing a prank. Anyway, now that this has happened to Yuta Gamon, what will he do? He might not do what I would do, you know! Yuta Gamon is special. He's been chosen! He might admit the reality of his death, and use it to do whatever he wanted as a ghost! Maybe he could make a harem for himself like you often see in light novels! That might actually improve sales! (lol) Anyway, look forward to Volume 3 to find out.

Tell me on Twitter what you think! Poya-ya!

—Chiyomaru Shikura